THE
MISTLETOE
BRIDE

& *other* HAUNTING TALES

Kate MOSSE

Illustrations by
ROHAN DANIEL EASON

An Orion paperback

First published in Great Britain in 2013
by Orion Books.
This paperback edition published in 2014
by Orion Books,
an imprint of The Orion Publishing Group Ltd,
Orion House, 5 Upper St Martin's Lane,
London WC2H 9EA

An Hachette UK company

1 3 5 7 9 10 8 6 4 2

A CIP catalogue record for this book is available from the British Library.

ISBN 978-1-4091-4906-4

Printed in Great Britain by Clays Ltd, St Ives plc

The Orion Publishing Group's policy is to use papers that
are natural, renewable and recyclable products and made
from wood grown in sustainable forests. The logging and
manufacturing processes are expected to conform to the
environmental regulations of the country of origin.

www.orionbooks.co.uk

Kate Mosse is the author of three works of non-fiction, three plays and six novels, including the number one multi-million international bestselling Languedoc Trilogy – *Labyrinth*, *Sepulchre* and *Citadel* – which was published to outstanding reviews and sold in more than 40 countries throughout the world in 38 languages. As well as historical fiction, Kate also writes ghost stories including *The Winter Ghosts* – also a number one bestseller – and *The Mistletoe Bride & Other Haunting Tales*, confirming her position as one of our most captivating storytellers. In recognition of her services to literature, Kate was awarded an OBE in the Queen's Birthday Honours List in June 2013. To find out more visit www.katemosse.co.uk

To Greg and Martha and Felix

CONTENTS

Foreword

I expect to pass through this world but once;
any good thing therefore that I can do,
or any kindness that I can show to any fellow human being,
let me do it now; let me not defer nor neglect it,
for I shall not pass this way again.

ETIENNE DE GRELLET DU MABILLIER

Like most novelists, over the years I've been asked to contribute short stories to magazines and anthologies. Some books are intended as pure entertainment, others to celebrate an anniversary or a season or in aid of a charity. Often the request is accompanied by an assumption that most writers will have stories squirrelled away, just waiting for a good home.

That was never true for me. I didn't start on short stories and graduate to novel writing, rather I came at it the other way around. Each time I was asked if I had anything, I knew my literary bottom drawer was empty. So I always started from scratch and discovered how much I enjoyed the challenge of writing self-contained short stories.

The novels in my Languedoc Trilogy – *Labyrinth, Sepulchre*

and *Citadel* – took years to research and years to write, so it was fun (and a relief) to work on a more intimate scale. I loved the need to capture a moment of experience, rather than creating a whole world and everything in it; I enjoyed being able to concentrate on one or two characters rather than wrestle with a cast of dozens, even hundreds; I enjoyed the slim time between having the idea and putting the last full stop on the page.

The Mistletoe Bride & Other Haunting Tales is my first collection of short stories. Of the fourteen, six have been published elsewhere before – though I have expanded or edited them for this edition. The other eight are new, either inspired by a particular time and place – in particular the landscape of Sussex, Hampshire, Brittany and the Languedoc – or by English and French folklore and legend. There are traditional ghost stories – spirits coming back from the dead to seek revenge, lost souls haunting the place where they died, white ladies and phantom hitchhikers – and also gentler tales about loss and grief or guilt. Some are first-person narratives and others told in the third person. What they have in common is a protagonist in a state of crisis, someone whose emotional state makes them more susceptible to experiences or happenings outside everyday life. They are women and men who, for a moment at least, have slipped between the cracks of the physical world we can see and understand and into a shadow world that may not even exist.

My first play, *Syrinx*, is also included. Since its premiere in 2009, it has become a popular piece for amateur groups to perform. There has been, until now, no printed script available.

Finally, I have written a brief Author's Note for each piece, giving the context and original inspiration – the narrative of the narrative – for those who're interested in how stories move from head to page. For me, one of the joys of putting together the collection was seeing a microcosm of the themes, ideas and styles I was to develop later in *Labyrinth*, *Sepulchre*, *Citadel* and *The Winter Ghosts*.

Any collection of work written over many years must, by its very nature, tell another story too – of how the author came to be the author she or he is. This, then, is mine.

Kate Mosse
Sussex, May 2013

THE MISTLETOE BRIDE

Bramshill House, Hampshire
October 1935

The Mistletoe Bride

At length an old chest that had long lain hid
Was found in the castle; they raised the lid,
And a skeleton form lay mouldering there,
In the bridal wreath of that lady fair.
Refrain: Oh, the mistletoe bough,
Oh, the mistletoe bough.

from 'The Mistletoe Bough'
THOMAS HAYNES BAYLY

I hear someone coming.

Has someone caught the echo of my footsteps on these floorboards? It is possible. It has happened before. I pause and listen, but now I no longer hear anything. I sigh. As always, hope is snatched away before it can take root.

Even now, after so long, I cannot account for the fact that no one ever ventures into this part of the house. I do not understand how I am still waiting, waiting after all these years. Sometimes I see them moving around below. Sense their presence. Bramshill House has been home to many families in my time and, though the clothes and the styles and the customs are different, it seems to me that each generation is much the same. I remember them all, their faces alive with the legends of the house and the belief that it is haunted. Men and women and children, listening to the stories. The story of a game of hide-and-seek.

I pray that this will be the day. The end of my story. That, this time, someone at last will find me. But the halls and the corridors beneath me are silent again.

No one is coming.

And so then, as always, I am carried back to that first December so very long ago.

*

It is my wedding day. I should be happy, and I am.

I am happy, yet I confess I am anxious too. My father's friends are wild. Their cups clashing against one another and goose fat glistening on their cheeks and their voices raised. There has been so much wine drunk that they are no longer themselves. There is a lawlessness in the glint of their eyes, though they are not yet so far gone as to forget their breeding and manners. Their good cheer echoes around the old oak hall, so loud that I can no longer hear the lute or viol or citole set for our entertainment.

There is mistletoe and holly, white berries and red.

At the end of the table, I see my beloved father and my face softens. He is proud of me and what this alliance will bring. Two local families of equal stature and worth, this union will be good for both. My mother has told me time and again how fortunate I am to be betrothed – married, as of three hours past – to a man who loves me and who is mindful of my worth.

And see how we sit together, at the head of the feast, to toast the goodly company.

I look to my husband.

Lovell is lively and bright. He touches my hand and compliments my dress, admires my blue eyes and the Christmas decorations that grace the hall. And he – I must learn to call him husband – dances well and speaks well and makes each man believe that he, of all of my father's guests, is the most welcome.

The scent of lilies, lily of the valley, though I do not understand how such blooms survive in the cold of this December.

I have been told Lovell has done great service to the Crown. He is said to be brave and that he acquitted himself in the wars, but yet the new Queen does not favour him. I do not know how this matters, if at all. In any case, today all affairs of state are forgotten. Lovell has opened Bramshill House to all those who should be here, regardless of their allegiance, and my father approves. This house that will, in time, become my home.

The wedding feast continues late into the afternoon, as was the custom then.

Things are different now.

Conviviality, the best of hospitality, there is food and wine enough to satisfy even the greediest of his guests. *Our* guests, I tell myself, though the word sits heavy in my mouth. I must learn to wear my new responsibilities more lightly.

The servants have gone back and forth, back and forth, with flagons and plates and dishes. No one lacks for anything. We have sung and listened to ballads of the old times, songs of love and loss and battle. And we have danced and danced, until my feet are sore and my slippers worn through. Lovell calls me his 'fairy bride', as he leads me in the cotillion. Up and down and round and around we go. I am lighter than air, he says, barely there at all, and I can see this pleases him.

The hours pass.

Outside it has grown dark and I am weary, having sat at this table for too long. I would like to withdraw. I would like to rest a while, though I know I cannot. So I continue to offer smiles and nods and I listen to the old man sitting on my right, who wishes to talk of God and duty and has flecks of spittle in the corner of his mouth.

I look to Lovell again and I see that he, too, has tired of the feast. Our glances meet and he inclines his head. He is as hidebound by the traditions as am I.

All at once, I understand what I might do. I get to my feet.

'My lords, shall we have a game?' I say. 'A game of hide-and-seek, for all those who yet have strength in their legs?'

My husband laughs. Straight away, the atmosphere changes. It bristles and sharpens. The young men think of what mischief might be hidden in the shadows, the young women dream of who might come to find them. The old men and matrons shake their heads, look indulgently on their excitement and remember their own youth.

'We shall,' says Lovell, clapping his hands. 'A splendid suggestion. Only if, though, my beautiful wife will honour me with a kiss beneath the mistletoe before the game begins.'

I feel no aversion to the thought of his lips upon mine, though I would rather it not be a sport to be observed by the assembled company. But I oblige and I smile, tilt my face to his. A servant holds a bough over our heads.

The bargain is struck.

The watchers at the table applaud and roar their approval.

'Now, let the game begin,' I say. For this moment, I am *la fille coquette*. Charming and gay and entrancing. I can play this role. I can see Lovell's eyes upon me and know he means to be the one who discovers my hiding place. There is part of me that shrinks at the thought of it, but he is a gentle man.

My husband claps his hands again and all fall silent.

'The ladies shall hide first,' he commands. 'The gentlemen shall seek. We will give you to the count of . . .'

But I do not hear what he says because we are already running, lightly, from the hall. Laughing and glancing back over our shoulders. Silk and brocade, our pretty gowns painting the long corridors and cavernous spaces of Bramshill House the colours of the rainbow.

I hear the chorus of male voices counting.

'Twenty-five, twenty-six, twenty-seven . . .'

My companions, girls who have not been told how unlady-like it is to show such excitement, are in high spirits. Like me, they are grateful to be released from the table and the eyes, hands, of the old men. We chatter, each of us choosing a room, though we keep it secret. Young girls imagining the beau who might love them.

I think of my husband. That I am now a wife.

I take the main staircase. I do not yet know Bramshill House well – there are sixty rooms or more – and I do not want to lose my way.

'Thirty-eight, thirty-nine, forty.'

On the landing, I hesitate, unsure of where to go. I need to be well hidden, the game loses its charm else, but not so well concealed that Lovell loses patience in the search.

'Forty-seven, forty-eight, forty-nine.'

We are scattering in all directions, in our game of

hide-and-seek, and it is Christmas. The heels of our slippers tap on the wooden floors and the pearls on the hem of my dress, hand stitched over the weeks leading up to my wedding, knock against the wainscot.

I take the next flight of stairs, up to the second floor where the smaller bedrooms are to be found. Pearl on wood, silk on dust, my bridal gown is heavy and ornate, but it fits me well and I am not hampered by its weight. Along the upper gallery and into a bare room, clearly little used, with a pretty fleur-de-lis wallpaper.

Perhaps I have brought the scent of lilies with me, but I fancy there is the slightest perfume in this room too.

'Ninety-nine and one hundred.'

Their voices are faint this far up, but immediately men's heel echo in the old oak hall and there is laughter. Some call ou paying suit to their favourite – all the Annes and the Mary and the Janes.

I hesitate again, then step inside the room. There is no furr ture here save a substantial old oak chest set below the windc I walk closer. The wooden coffer is deep and long, the length a man, and bound fast by four wide metal bands. I wonder once held the trousseau of another bride brought to Brams House? Or do its proportions suggest it was made for a of the manor for a voyage? Strong and sturdy to protec owner's possessions from the roll and swell and jilt of the

Then I hear footsteps and remember the game.

I unbuckle the ornate metal fastening and lift the lid heavy, cumbersome and the clasp is loose and rattles, tho pay little heed to that. Rather, I am wondering if it might as my hiding place and, indeed, the chest is empty, sav bolt of pale blue cotton, which lines the bottom like a blanket. I think of how pleasant it would be to lie down and rest. Then I imagine Lovell's face as he opens the chest and sees me looking up at him, framed in lace and tulle, and my mind is made up.

I lift my bridal gown and, careful not to slip, I climb over and into the chest. I arrange my skirts around me and fold my veil to serve as a pillow, then lie back. I feel like a child again, not somebody's wife.

I hesitate for a third time. The chest is visible from the corridor, even in the weak light from the candles, and I do not want my hiding place to be too immediately evident. I reach up and, with both hands, I lower the lid shut. I hear the sigh of the wood as it drops, firm, back into place. The heavy click of the clasp.

I can hear the sounds of merriment from below, and know someone soon will come. Lovell, soon, will come.

Then I hear the sound of the door to the room banging shut, blown by a gust of wind. I do not think it will matter too much.

It is confined, within the chest, and I realise the air will soon become stale. I try the lid and, for a moment, feel a spark of concern that I cannot move it, but I feel safe within the dark and am grateful for the solitude. I am warm and comfortable and know the seekers soon will find me, so I do not worry.

I close my eyes and wait for Lovell.

*

I did not mean to sleep.

My head fills with strange dreams, wild imaginings that follow one hard on the heels of the next. A kaleidoscope of brightly coloured glass, becoming darker. Like candles on a cake being blown out, one by one by one. My sleep grows deeper. Memories of the springs and summers and autumns of childhood. A winter wedding of tulle and silk, the white of the mistletoe bough and the green of the holly decking the hall.

The food on the marriage table grows cold, congeals. They are looking and calling out my name. It is no longer a game. Impatience turns to fear.

Lovell does not find me.

They hunted all that night and the next day. They ventured to the highest reaches of the house, but if someone did step into the bare room with the fleur-de-lis wallpaper, they investigated no further. If they saw the chest, they saw it was locked fast from the outside and did not think I could be there. When they called my name and I did not answer, they moved on through corridors and the attics.

By then, I could no longer hear them. I felt no pain or fear at the moment of my passing, just a simple slipping away.

I died as I had lived. Quietly, gently, leaving little trace.

*

I discovered I could still see things, in the house and beyond its boundaries. I could hear things and sense the shifting of the world, even though I was no longer part of it.

They drained the pond and scoured every square of the three hundred acres, extending the search beyond the gates to the villages of Farley Hill and Eversley, Hazeley, Heckfield and Swallowfield. They dragged the rivers, running high and fast at that time of year, the Whitewater and the Blackwater, the Hart.

Still they did not find me.

The weeks turned to months, the months to years. Lovell lost hope. He took to wandering the roads and the pathways through the woods, crying my name, and I wept to see him so broken.

Inside my oak tomb, my body grew thin and, in time, faded quite away. All that was left were bones, wrapped in tulle and silk, resting on a bed of blue cotton. Knowing I would have no peace until I was laid in the ground, I despaired that I would never be found. That I would be condemned to this half existence for all time.

Lovell grew old.

The children sang rhymes about him and pitied him, though they feared him too. When he died, he was buried in the grounds of Bramshill House where we had hoped to make a home together. And although I never had the chance to know him in life, my longing to lie beside him in death grew stronger, sharper, with each year that passed.

I had possession of these corridors. From time to time, some could sense my company. Stories of a white winter lady glimpsed in the upper floors each December. Rumours of footsteps heard running in panic from room to room, the wedding guests of years ago in their desperate search for the mistletoe bride.

Yet though the house was known to be haunted, still no one came to carry me home.

*

The years marched on, from one generation unto the next.

England waged war in the East and in Africa. On the lawns

of Bramshill House, men played cricket and the white deer continued to roam the parkland. The story of Lovell and his fairy bride faded from memory. All those who remembered that night were long gone, their children and children's children moved away.

A new century began. England was at war once more, this time in Europe. The sons and fathers of the villages, where once my Lovell searched, were sent to die at Boar's Head and the Somme. With so many lying dead, how could the loss of one young bride so many years ago count for much? I heard tell that red poppies blossomed on the fields of Flanders and France where their bodies fell.

Here, each year, the berries of the mistletoe bough still bloomed white at Christmas and the leaves of the holly are green.

I continue to sleep.

*

When next I wake, it is summer.

Bramshill House has been sold. Since 1699, there have been Copes here. Now, the last of the family has relinquished his possession of the estate and its three hundred acres of land. Soon, a new owner will come and another story will begin.

The last of the boxes are going today. I can hear the footsteps on the gravel and a strange thrumming sound, the vibrating of an engine. No horses now, but rather rubber wheels and the ability to travel great distances.

These things I see and I don't see.

The echo of my heart starts to beat faster. They are making a final sweep of the house, moving from room to room. Now

I can hear someone outside my door. Men's voices – always men's voices – searching and asking for instructions.

I catch the memory of my breath.

The door to the room is opening, I hear its judder as the wood sticks on the floor, then releases itself and swings back. This is the sound I have prayed for. Footsteps crossing the bare floorboards, coming towards me. Hands resting on the old oak chest.

It is too heavy for one man to move. I hear him grunt with the effort, then call for assistance. Now other footsteps. Four feet, not two. Then, I feel the lurch and heave as the chest is picked up, lower at my feet, higher at my head. Like a ship at sea, it rocks to and fro as they try to find purchase, but the weight and bulk defeats them. They cannot hold it. A curse, a shout, fingers slipping.

I am falling.

One end goes down and I am thrown sideways, an odd lurching sensation as the chest hits the floor with a thud. The metal gives, the clasp breaks and the lid, finally, cracks open.

At last.

A moment of silence, then one of the men screams. He shouts for help as he runs from the room. Gibbering about a skeleton in a bridal gown, bones tumbling out of an old oak chest.

I am smiling.

*

Now I can smell lilies of the valley once more.

And I can feel the sweet memory of happiness and I re-member what it was to laugh and to love and to hope. My smile grows stronger as I think of my husband and how soon – after so very long – we shall be reunited.

Lovell and his mistletoe bride.

Author's Note

When I was little, my parents had a book – *Folklore, Myths and Legends of Britain*. Published by Reader's Digest in 1973, it had a black cloth cover and a gold embossed image of a Viking, with beard and horned helmet. Inside, a cornucopia of stories that had endured for two thousand years. Divided into three sections – the 'Lore of Britain', the 'Romance of Britain' and 'People of Myth' – I was so entranced with the book, I flirted with the idea of applying to read Folklore Studies at university instead of English. My parents – sensibly – took no notice and the moment passed.

And yet . . .

It was in *Folklore, Myths and Legends of Britain* that I first came across the story of 'The Mistletoe Bride'. Several places in Britain claimed to be the historical setting for the story – Skelton in Yorkshire, Minster Lovell Hall in Oxfordshire, Marwell Old Hall in Hampshire, Castle Horneck in Cornwall, Exton Hall in Rutland, Brockdish Hall in Norfolk, and Bawdrip Rectory and Shapwick in Somerset. The Cope family of Bramshill House claimed to be able to produce the famous oak chest, in which the young bride was supposed to have suffocated. Grisly, oddly compelling, it is the sort of story that sticks in the imagination.

The story of the Mistletoe Bride first appeared in 1823 as a blank verse poem, 'Ginevra', in Samuel Rogers' book *Italy*. He made claim for the story to be 'founded on fact, though the time and the place are uncertain.' However, its popularity can be laid at the door of the nineteenth-century songwriter Thomas Haynes Bayly, who set the story to music by H. R. Bishop, and published it as 'The Mistletoe Bough' in his 1844 volume *Songs, Ballads and Other Poems*. It was an instant hit and became one of the most popular Victorian and Edwardian Christmas music hall songs.

My parents' book is long gone. I managed, some years later, to find an old replacement copy which sits now – the spine missing and in pride of place – in my study where I write. In idle moments, I take it down and let it fall open at a page of its own choosing. Lose myself for an hour or two.

In memory of those long and happy teenage days reading back in the 1970s, I wrote two versions of the story of the bride who vanished on her wedding day for this collection. This, the first of them – a 'white lady' story – is dedicated to my wonderful mother and my beloved father, who died in 2011.

DUET

Pinewalk Heights, Bournemouth

October 1965

Duet

True! – nervous – very, very dreadfully nervous I had been and am; but why *will* you say that I am mad? The disease had sharpened my senses – not destroyed – not dulled them. Above all was the sense of hearing acute. I heard all things in the heaven and in the earth. I heard many things in hell. How then am I mad?

from 'The Tell-Tale Heart'
EDGAR ALLAN POE

'It was the smell.'

'The smell?' I say.

'No reason for it and, to tell you the truth, I didn't notice it, not at first. I was that busy. Working all the hours God sent, looking for a promotion. First step on the ladder. And I had a girl – nothing serious, but nice enough. Willing enough, if you know what I mean – so I wasn't much home.' He stops to sigh. He enjoys sighing. 'Those days, I did all the right things. Fitted in. Making my way, then. Going up in the world.'

I nod. 'Yes.'

He meets my eye, then his gaze slips away again. Embarrassed, though here there's no need for that. Within this room, there's no need to worry about what people might think. Past all of that now. He licks dry lips. Another glance that slips over me and away. Easier like that. Less personal.

'So, what with one thing and another, I was barely there. That's the situation. Why I hadn't got around to it.'

I nod again. 'Yes.'

'On the up, I was. Had big plans. So, yes, as I was saying, what with one thing and another, I hadn't got round to moving the stuff down to the cellar. After he'd gone—'

'Who'd gone?' I ask, just to keep the story on the straight and narrow.

'Man in Number Three. Turner.' He pauses, to check that I'm following. 'She was that put out, his things got dumped in the hall and left. He had no relatives.'

'How do you know?' I ask.

He's shocked by the question, surprised at us varying from our script, and he's right to be. It is a new question. I've never asked it before, but we need to make progress today. He considers, then answers.

'Stands to reason, doesn't it? If there'd been anybody, they'd have got in touch. Come to see what was theirs by rights. He had no children, she told me that. No brothers or sisters. She put something in the paper, but not a soul turned up. No one. Stands to reason.' He pauses, as another thought jabs at him. 'His "effects", the lawyer called them.'

I can think of all sorts of reasons why no one but he and the landlady knew the old man in Number Three was gone, but it's not my place to argue. My job is to listen. Prompt, from time to time, but only as and when.

'What sort of things, these "effects"?' I mime the speech marks, intending to set him and me against the sort of jumped-up phrases the lawyers use. The trick doesn't work. He doesn't join in. He doesn't want to be on my side. There's no 'us' in his mind.

Instead, the same slippery glance.

'Such as, such as . . .' He stops and it's not a pause, as if he's working out what to say next, but more the kind of deep silence that means he's withdrawn from the conversation. I wonder if I've strayed too far from our usual script, done things in the wrong order. Or triggered some new memory which is getting in the way of his story. The story that matters. But then he meets my eye and I realise he's grateful for the chance to speak about other things first. Not what happened in the cellar.

'An oil painting,' he says. 'A village in the Pyrenees, I reckon it was. Turns out Turner spent the summers back in the day bicycling around France.'

He's talking fast now, the words tumbling over one another. 'Mrs Nash told me. Wouldn't have thought that to see him. Gone to seed, if you know what I mean.'

I nod, but choose not to speak. I don't want to disturb the fragile balance. And it was the right decision because he carries on, now letting the words run away with him.

'Worked at the same firm, man and boy. Forty years, give or take.'

'Give or take,' I nod. 'I like that.'

He smiles, then clears his throat to disguise the fact he's pleased with the compliment. 'It's what Mrs Nash said.'

'What did Mr Turner do then, this job of his?'

He pauses, then shrugs. 'Never talked to him myself more than to pass the time of day.'

'No?'

'No,' he says loudly. Sharp, now. Annoyed, now. 'The odd "how do" or "turned out nice again", on the stairs, that's all.'

'You and he, you weren't what you'd call friends. Pals.'

He shakes his head. 'He was up on the second floor. I had the ground floor. Nice enough room, own sink and a hotplate. Had to share a toilet, but it was always clean, I'll give her that. I look out over the esplanade. Nice in summer, day trippers coming and going.'

'Better in the autumn,' I offer. 'Quiet.'

'Quiet.' He nods. 'That's it, quiet.'

He runs his hands over his hair, fingers pushing hard into his skull, then shakes them out. Flicking imaginary drops of water into the space between us. He licks his lips.

'All right for some. The rest of us slaving away.'

He stops and stares at me and, though I'm not sure if he's talking about the tenant in Number Three or Mrs Nash or someone else altogether, I realise he's waiting for a response.

'You said it.' I pull a man-of-the-world face. 'All right for some.'

'All right for some, you can say that again. Never a truer word spoken.'

Now he's smiling, but the smile never reaches his eyes. There's something off about his expression, calculating, as if he's tricked me. Got me on the run. But it's hard to be sure and I don't want to judge. Not my job to judge. My job is to listen. Let him do the talking.

'You're telling me, you're telling me,' he says, 'never a truer word spoken. I like that.' He stops. Takes a breath. Lets his shoulders drop. 'I like that.'

He starts picking at a thread on the sleeve of his jacket, a heavy twill much too warm for the overheated room we're sitting in. The picking turns to scratching. Now he's rubbing at the material as if trying to rub away the weave, faster and faster.

'Lucky sod,' he says, 'lucky lucky lucky—'

I can't let him drift away from me, so I jump in. 'As well as the painting, what else?'

My voice is loud and he's startled, of course he is. It's not like me to raise my voice. His head jerks up and he stares, blind eyes seeing something else. Not me. I can feel him slipping out of my company again.

'I didn't mean to upset you,' I say quickly. 'I'm sorry.'

He doesn't acknowledge the apology. He's still staring, looking right through me, but then the moment passes and he swallows. His Adam's apple bobs. His skin there is sore and red, raw. I raise my hand to my throat in sympathy, imagining the cold water in the bowl and how the old razor, blunt through lack of use, stings and, for a moment, we are the same, him and me.

'I was wondering what else was in the box,' I say.

Now his eyes focus and he is laughing, embarrassed again now, and we are both returned to this hot and claustrophobic room, with the fixed table and everything painted that same green. The bed and the radiator that knocks and the clock that ticks and the words that rattle between us, turning the air black.

'The painting, I told you about the painting? I don't know much about art, but it didn't look up to much. No more than average. What else? A pair of cufflinks. Silver plate, nice if you like that sort of thing. A carriage clock. Engraved. Retirement, that sort of thing. But it . . .'

He's seeing the box in his mind's eye, the size and the shape of it. The way it blocked the hall in the drab boarding house. Then he's remembering the smell. Cupping his hands over his nose, breathing in stale air. And he does not want to go further, though that's the reason we are here.

'. . . the smell,' he says. 'There was no reason for it.' His hands are fluttering again. 'Outspan oranges.'

'Written on the side, yes you told me,' I say. I know all of this. It's what comes after that's the mystery.

He closes his eyes. 'If it hadn't been for the smell . . .' And he says it again and again, as he presses his hands between his knees, palm to palm, as if praying, though there is no peace here. 'My fault.'

Now he is rocking backwards and forwards. This too is a new development and I don't like it. Even so, I notice the plucked threads on his sleeve, caught in the pale November sun coming in through the small locked window, set high up in the wall. A sickly yellow light. I rub the sleeve of my jacket in sympathy and pull the snagged thread.

'So you moved the box, as soon as you had the time,' I said. 'Like you promised, moved it from the hall.'

He shakes his head. 'Couldn't leave it there.'

This part of our duet is familiar too. We've had this part of our conversation before. The damp hall, the stale October air, the raincoats on the hooks by the door and the lino peeling, the table with its layer of dust and bills mounting up, the front doormat grown bald with years of boots and wiped soles and sand. But we haven't gone further. We've got no further than the top of the cellar stairs.

'Her legs are bad. Can't get up and down the stairs, too steep. Never went down there.'

I swallow.

'Too much for her,' he says again. 'Mrs Nash. Not been down there for years.'

'So why that day?' I say. This, when all's said and done, is what I want to know. 'What was special about that day in particular?'

'I told you.' Stubborn, this time. Resentful. 'The smell. Getting worse.' He looks up at me, then away. 'Every time I went past, couldn't ignore it.'

For a moment, there's silence. I wonder if he's going to stop here. Sometimes, he wants to talk. Other times, he clams up.

'It was a Thursday,' I say.

'Yes.' He takes the bait. 'Thurs – day,' he says, two staccato beats. Today, there is something living and breathing in the word. The whole story contained there, in that moment, and I think we might be getting somewhere.

'Mrs Nash goes to the bingo Thursdays, isn't that right?'

He doesn't answer. His gaze slips away from me and towards the world outside the room and he starts mumbling. 'Slip, slide, perish, cannot take the strain. Slip, slip, slide, perish.'

I'm caught on the hop this time, I admit it. Coming out with poetry. He's never struck me as the type. Never done it before.

'Thomas Sterns,' he says, 'that's what T. S. stands for. Not many people know that.' And he's smiling the same sly smile because he thinks he's bested me. Won another round. '*Four Quartets.*'

'I know,' I snap, though I shouldn't let my feelings show.

His face is ablaze with cunning. He wags a finger at me. Points. 'But which one? Guess. Air, Water, Earth, Fire? Guess.'

I can't indulge him any further in this. It's no good for him, can't be. Won't get us anywhere.

'Why didn't she go to the bingo that Thursday?'

My voice is level, but there's enough displeasure in it and he hears and withdraws again, angry I'm not playing along. The praying hands, the bowed head, the crumpled shoulders, the swallowing and swallowing. My throat is dry too.

For an age, he is silent. The room is heavy with disappointment, with misunderstanding. He feels I have let him down and he might be right, but it can't be helped. We need to get somewhere. Make progress. The water gurgles in the old iron radiator. Beyond the door, the monotonous rattle of a trolley and the slide of a bolt somewhere further along the corridor.

We don't have much time.

I swallow. 'Why didn't Mrs Nash go to bingo that Thursday?'

'She did,' he says, sullen again. 'Forgot her purse. Came back.'

'Or she guessed.'

'No.'

He shrugs, the shifty fidget of a child. A quick up and down of the shoulders. Guilt? Is it guilt? I can't tell. Feigning uninterest, certainly.

I help him on his way. A firm hand in the small of the back. 'She was suspicious, wasn't she? Pretended to go, then came back to spy on you.'

'It wasn't my fault.'

'No.' I change tack. 'An accident, when all's said and done. Her fault, not yours. Stairs were too steep.'

And he looks at me for a moment with such gratitude that I feel happy. Actually happy.

'She'd no cause to go on at me all the time,' he says. 'I said I'd move the box, just not got round to it, but . . . the smell, you see. Like seaweed or fish. Rotting fish. Thought it was coming from the box, she did.'

'But it wasn't.'

'No.'

I look him in the eye. 'So then what happened?'

I say it quietly and carefully, but it doesn't work and he shakes his head, sent spiralling back to the beginning again. The bare bones of the story are the same – the tenant in Number Three going off, Mrs Nash asking him to clear out the room, the box sitting in the hall with the carriage clock and the painting of the Pyrenees. This time, though, no funeral and no lawyer. The brown envelope spilling money. Fifty-quid notes.

I'm getting impatient. 'So,' I say, 'the twenty-first of October, Thursday, you decide to do it.' I clap my hands and he jumps. 'That's it. Just like that, you decide today's the day to make good on your promise. Pick up the box and you see all that money, yes? Been there all along. Put it in the pocket of your trousers, yes? Then you open the door down to the cellar. Yes? The paint's peeling, isn't it, chipped? You promised you'd have a look at that too, didn't you?'

He frowns. 'She was always on at me,' he says. 'Never gave it a rest, all the time on at me.'

'So you open the door, yes, and you look down, but it's too gloomy to see anything. Isn't it, isn't that right? You can't see anything down there, so you don't know what's down there. You put out your hand, feel around, looking for a light switch.'

'Wired wrong. Upside down.'

'But you do find the switch. Flick it up. Sickly yellow light down there.'

'Sickly yellow light.'

I nod. 'And straight away, you know there's something wrong down there, don't you?' I lean forward. 'You can smell it, can't you? Smell of the sea. Of rotting fish.'

He puts his hands over his ears. He doesn't want to hear any more. He is seeing it all now, smelling it, remembering the cold on his bare skin and the dust and the cobwebs, the decay and damp of a cellar in a seaside town. He doesn't want to be back at that cellar on that Thursday the twenty-first of October 1965.

But that's why he's here. Why we are here.

'Not blood,' he says, 'it was a sweet smell.'

'You didn't think it would be so bad, did you? You rolled up your sleeves – didn't want to spoil that pullover.'

'Oranges . . .' he whispers.

'You pick up the box and carry it down,' I say, pushing him further. 'Know you've got to do something before she gets back. The smell's too bad down there. She's bound to notice.'

'Ten steps down.'

'Eight,' I correct him. 'Quite a weight, that box. All that stuff in it. Three or four trophies, a shield with his name on it. Bowls, wasn't it?'

He's shaking his head, sticking to the first story. 'Painting and a carriage clock and cuff links and the money.'

'There all along,' I say.

He is shaking his head. 'There all along. Thought it was under the mattress.' His voice drops to a whisper. 'Why did she come back? She'd never have known. We would have been all right.'

'The box was heavy,' I say.

I see his expression. He's frightened at how much I know, how much he has already told me. He is staring at me, clear brown eyes, a little yellow. Medication yellow.

'I could manage.'

I admire his courage, but I can't let myself be deflected. 'You have dust on your cuffs, and that annoys you. It's your best shirt and you need it for the weekend.'

He nods. 'The Gaumont. Saturday night.'

'The girl, yes,' I say, impatiently. We are doing well, but we have to stay in the house. I can't let him get away from me. We have to go down into the cellar, him and me. Only then will the last pieces of the jigsaw fall into place.

'So you managed, of course you did. Strong chap like you. On the up.' I hesitate. 'But she came back. Called out, didn't she?'

'Caught me by surprise.'

'That's right, so you slipped. Lost your footing.'

He flushes. 'It was dark.'

'Of course it was. Could have happened to anyone, in the dark.'

'She shouldn't have come back.'

'That's right.'

'She scared me.'

'That's right,' I say. 'Her fault really. If she'd left well alone.'

'Her fault.'

I can see beads of sweat on his forehead, a sickly yellow. Skin sickly yellow. Or is that Turner? Lying on the floor of the cellar, like a dummy. One of those mannequins in Reynolds department store on the front. I pull the handkerchief from my pocket and wipe my face. He does the same – great minds think alike – and he looks better for it.

I put my handkerchief away. 'That's when she saw him. Over your shoulder, looking over your shoulder.'

'Screamed.'

'No call for it,' I say.

He's nodding. 'I didn't mean to hurt her. Tried to explain.'

'But she starts screaming, that's the thing, says she's going to call the police.'

'I reach up, just wanted to talk to her. Got hold of her ankle.'

I shudder, remembering the saggy nylons like loose skin on her leg, the sponge-like flesh beneath. Her tumbling down the wooden steps, taking us both down with her. The box and the silver plate rattling down to the cellar floor. The weight of her lying on top of me. Not waking up.

'Banged my head,' he says. 'Out for the count.'

'It wasn't your fault,' I say. 'Bad luck she came home. She didn't have to scream.'

'She didn't have to make such a fuss. I only wanted to explain.'

'You're telling me, you're telling me,' I say, 'never a truer word spoken. I like that.' I stop. Take a breath. Let my shoulders drop. 'I like that.'

I start picking at a thread on the sleeve of my jacket, a heavy twill much too warm for our room. There's blood on the sleeve, that's the thing. All that money. All that money stashed away. Thought it was under the mattress in Number Three. He found me looking. I didn't mean to hurt him, but Turner went for me. Pushed him. Hit his head. Down he went. Taking him down to the cellar, knew he'd be safe there. Mrs Nash never went down there, couldn't manage the steps.

If she hadn't have come back, she'd never have known.

'Never a truer word spoken,' I say.

There's a noise at the door. The sound of the key being turned in the lock and the bolt being shot back. We are out of time.

The orderlies come in. Tweedledee and Tweedledum, we call them, on account of their size.

'All right, Jim? Time for your medication.'

I let my eyes slip away, warning him not to say anything in front of them. Not to admit to anything. It's not murder if you don't mean to kill someone. Turner or Mrs Nash, not his fault.

Checking he's quiet now. And he is. He's sitting silent as the dead in the corner of the room, not saying a word. I put my finger to my lips just in case. They can't see him. They don't know he's here.

'Yes, I'm all right,' I say.

'Here you go then.'

I hold out my hand obediently. The quicker it's done, the quicker they'll go and we can get back to business. Tweedledee drops two yellow pills into my palm. Sickly yellow. I take the paper cup and swallow, drain the water and hand the cup back. Tweedledum ticks something on his list, then they are wheeling the trolley out of the room again.

'Someone be round with supper soon,' he says.

I put my hands over my nose, keen for them to be gone so we can resume our conversation. I can't believe they can't smell it. The rotting fish, the seaweed. Just like before. I want them to go. We're at the interesting part now. The reason we're here.

'See you tomorrow,' says Tweedledee.

'Tomorrow it is,' I say.

I wait for the bolt again and the key again, then I turn round.

'Thought they'd never go,' I say. 'Now, where were we?'

But he's gone. I'm on my own. Pity. A pity.

I lie back on the bed. It doesn't matter though. We'll talk again tomorrow. Start again. Get to the bottom of things to-morrow. I must ask to do something about the smell. The rotting fish, the seaweed. Someone's going to notice soon. Someone's bound to notice. I look around for the box, but that's gone too.

He's taken it. Perhaps he's already taken it down to the cellar.

'Tomorrow it is then,' I murmur. 'Never a truer word spoken. All right for some, all right for some.'

Author's Note

When I started 'Duet', I had in my mind to write a doppel-gänger story. Literally meaning 'double walker' in German, a doppelgänger is a shadow self – a living ghost – supposed to be someone's double. In traditional ghost stories, it is only the owner of the doppelgänger who can see this phantom self and is often – usually – a harbinger of death. In stories of bi-location, a person can either spontaneously or willingly project his or her double, known as a 'wraith', to a remote location. This double is indistinguishable from the real person and can interact with others just as the real person would.

However, during the writing process, things went their own way and it became a story about conscience. Like Lady Macbeth being unable to wash her hands clean of Duncan's blood or the murderer in Edgar Allan Poe's 'The Tell-Tale Heart' – who imagines he can hear the heart of the old man he's killed beating under the floor and so gives himself away – guilt exacts a heavy price.

The story also seemed to belong in the 1960s, an era of land-ladies and oddball misfits living in a seaside town where events might go unnoticed for some time.

RED LETTER DAY

Montségur, the French Pyrenees
March 2001

Red Letter Day

And Something's odd – within –
That person that I was –
And this One – do not feel the same –
Could it be Madness – this?

Poem 410
EMILY DICKINSON

It was a mistake to take the mountain road into the Pyrenees. On the map it had looked more direct and, having made up her mind, Claire wanted to take the quickest route, before her courage deserted her and she conjured up an excuse not to go. To put it off again.

This journey had been more than three years in the making. Claire didn't want to cause any more distress and upset to those friends and family who'd done their best to look after her and help her get through things. It would get better, they told her. She'd never forget him, but it wouldn't always feel this bad. Perhaps she'd have another child. Time, they said, was a great healer.

If anything, the passing of one year to the next had made her grief more acute, her sense of loss more profound. Memories of the tiny, lifeless body in his cot, the weight of her son in her arms, the look of him. She knew things would never get better. Her heart would never heal and nor did she want it to.

With that acceptance had come relief, then a sense of purpose. All she wanted was not to feel anything, not to think anything, to close her eyes and see only white space. There was no point going on.

The decision made things easier. The place had been harder to choose. Claire wanted it be somewhere away from her everyday life, so as not to burden her family and friends, and somewhere remote.

Then, it came to her. Years ago, they'd gone on holiday to south-west France, the Ariège, where her mother's family had originally come from. Holed up in her tiny hotel in Carcassonne, guide book in hands, Claire had been captivated by the story of the Cathars. Had fallen in love with the tragic history of Montségur, the mountain citadel in the Pyrenees where a generation of rebels and heretics had made their final stand nearly eight hundred years before. One of her own ancestors among them.

Why not there?

According to legend, Montségur was the Holy Mountain of Grail legend. Or maybe the inspiration for Wagner's *Parsifal*, *Munsalvaesche*. Or a blueprint for the Mount of Salvation, *Mons Salvationis*. A place of hope and revelation and salvation. A place to live and to die.

It was a place of myth, certainly. The ruined fortress perched impossibly high above the village of Montségur, three sides of the castle hewn out of the mountainside itself. Many different citadels, different strongholds had been constructed on that same inhospitable spot, their rise and fall testament to the turbulent history of the Ariège. *Mont Ségur*, the safe mountain. The spirit of place, however, remained constant.

The idea took root until Montségur was the only place Claire could imagine feeling at peace.

Today was Thursday, 16th March. She'd picked the date deliberately. It was the anniversary of the day in 1244 when the defeated inhabitants of the citadel finally came down from their mountain retreat. Two hundred Cathar believers – heretics in the eyes of the Catholic Church – had chosen death by fire rather than to recant their faith. Ordinary believers and their priests, men and women both. Their remaining friends and families were brought before the Inquisition to bear witness to the horror of the times. Forced to listen to the screaming as those they loved died, to see the poisonous black cloud rising from the pyre. Covered their noses and mouths to keep out the sickly sweet stench of burning flesh.

Claire shook her head. Today was not the day for such violent images, she'd lived with those long enough. Today was a red letter day, the sort of day to be picked out in gold leaf and crimson ink on parchment. Today, she would stand in the place where – in the poet's words – prayer had been valid, and make her choice. Many times over the past three years she had pictured herself climbing the mountain, her feet steady on the flat slippery stones, her breath white in the chill air.

Time, now, to make the journey.

*

As Claire left Carcassonne, driving south towards the mountains, the air was soft and the dawn sky a gentle pink. A perfect spring day, though the hotel proprietor warned her that it would be winter still in the mountains. The clock on the dashboard of her hire car blinked out the time: 8:00.

She had headed first for Limoux – beautiful in summer with its central square and rocky river winding through the town – then on towards Couiza. The sun grew weaker, less definite. At Puivert, the pale spring mist turned to rain. Now, as she turned off onto the mountain road, following a signpost for Montségur, the rain was turning to sleet.

The narrow strip of tarmac twisted and turned back on itself until Claire felt carsick and dizzy and disorientated. As she climbed higher and higher, the temperature dropped.

Sleet turned to hail.

*

After three hours of driving, Claire reached the village of Montségur. Snow was hitting the windscreen and visibility was down to a few metres. The mountain, towering over the village, was half shrouded in a mantle of thick grey cloud, and the citadel itself was invisible.

Claire swapped driving shoes for her old hiking boots, the fur flattened by years of service, then got out of the car. Her feet crunched on the shards of ice on the ground. All other sound was muffled. She saw wisps of smoke winding out of one or two chimneys, evidence of the presence of others behind shuttered doors. She thought she heard a dog bark, although the sound was quickly swallowed by the billowing fog that prowled between the buildings. All she could be sure of was her own breath, white in the cold air, and her footsteps echoing through empty village streets.

Everything was closed. There were no other visitors and nobody local was unwise enough to be out. Whichever direction she faced, she seemed to be heading into a biting wind. Regretting her lack of hat and gloves, Claire pulled her red duffel coat tight around her. She always felt cold these days in any case. Friends thought it was because she was thin, but she knew the chill was inside her and that no amount of wool or fleece would make any difference to that.

She pushed her hands deeper into her pockets and walked on, drawn by the promise of a lighted window up ahead. The sign outside the restaurant was banging rhythmically against the wall, a monotonous thud of wood against stone.

It was too early for lunch, but the sign said OUVERT and when she pushed the door, Claire found it was unlocked. She stepped inside. Warm air rushed to greet her, rubbing against her cold hands and cheeks. She stamped the snow from her boots, then paused.

Something didn't seem right.

Claire stood still in the small entrance hall, until she realised what it was. There was no noise, nothing. No clatter of pans, or babble of conversation. There was no smell of food cooking.

'Hello?'

Nothing but the echo of her own voice surged back at her.

Pushing her hood back from her head, Claire shook her dark hair free. For years she had worn it in a sharp geometric bob – blunt fringe, blunt edges resting just above her shoulders – every photo the same: school, graduation, wedding. Then, three years ago when everything ceased to matter, she stopped bothering. Her black hair was long now, lifeless.

'*Il y a quelqu'un?*'

No one answered. She walked up a couple of steps, then paused and called out again:

'*Allô? Vous servez, oui?*'

Now she was at the top of the stairs. Claire found she was standing in a large, pleasant dining room. Exposed stone walls and wooden beams and floors, a timeless room. It felt welcoming, friendly even, despite the fact it was empty. A fire burned fiercely in the hearth. To her left there was a long wooden bar, the bottles and glasses gleaming. The centre of the room was filled with rows of waxed refectory tables, each seating ten and laid for lunch. Knives and forks, bowls of salt, oil and vinegar. Earthenware pitchers of water up the middle of each table and small matching bowls, in place of glasses, face down at each setting.

'*S'il vous plaît?*' Claire said loudly.

Still, nothing. She went into the kitchen, peered through the glass in the door, and saw no one. She hesitated, then walked in to the deserted space. The oven was hot, though, and there was the lingering smell of cooking. Thyme, perhaps? Red wine and onions? Claire peered out of a small, square window to a stone yard below, but there were no signs of life there either. No footsteps in the snow, no prints of a cat or a dog. If someone had recently gone that way, they had left no evidence of their presence.

On the counter, she noticed a round wooden board containing *chèvre*, a generous wedge of *cantal*, thick slabs of cured mountain ham and tomatoes. Next to it was a wicker basket of bread. She picked up a piece, then pulled off a corner and ate it. Fresh, *pain du matin* rather than yesterday's stale *baguette*. As if someone had known she was coming.

Claire looked at her watch and found it had stopped. She

tapped the face, but the hands were stuck at ten past eleven, about the time she'd arrived in Montségur. She hesitated, then, like Goldilocks, she took the food and went back into the dining room. No doubt the owner had simply nipped out to run some errand or another. She would settle with him when he came back.

She sat down at the table closest to the window. She could see her hire car, a layer of snow already covering the windscreen. Even if she decided not to go through with things, she had no choice but to stay in the village for the time being at least. She had no snow chains and no snow tyres.

Claire helped herself to a glass of red wine from a *demi-carafe* on the table, amazed to realise she was properly hungry, hungry for the first time in three years. Normal sensations, feelings, were coming back. She smiled. It seemed appropriate that here, at the top of the world, at the end of the world, her emotions should be thawing and coming back to life. She felt she had come home.

*

She must have dozed, though she had no memory of laying her head down on her arms at the table. She woke with a start, not sure who or what had disturbed her, only that something had.

For a moment, she felt calm. Then, the familiar weight on her chest once more as grief tapped her on the shoulder. Today, though, there was a sense of purpose too as she remembered where she was and why.

A red letter day, yes.

Claire stood up. The fire had burnt a little lower, her glass and plate were empty and the light was different. When she looked out, she saw the weather had cleared. The snow, sleet and mist had gone and now white clouds were scudding across a piercingly blue sky.

Claire was keen to be gone now, before she lost her nerve. She was surprised the owner still hadn't come back, but she left a twenty euro note on the table to cover her meal, then emptied the rest of the contents of her purse on the table. She had no more need of money and she wanted them to know – whoever *they* were – how much she appreciated their hospitality. That even in their absence, she had been made to feel welcome.

She hurried down the stairs and out into the cold, exhilarating air. Although still deserted, the streets were brighter and a pale sun cast shadows on the ground. Beyond the village, now Claire could see the citadel itself, high above the road, a grey castle set against the Pyrenean blue. She walked steadily, leaving the village behind her. Once or twice she thought she heard whispering, women's voices carried on the wind, but each time she turned, there was no one there.

She paused, breathless, at the foot of the mountain, to gather her strength for the climb. According to her guidebook the summit was nearly four thousand feet above sea level, so she would need to take it steadily and slowly. After all, there was no need to rush. Not now.

Claire slowly approached the Cathar memorial on the *Prats dels Cremats*, the Field of the Burned, which marked the place where the hundreds of Cathars had walked into the flames. The stone monument, a small *stèle*, was less imposing than she'd expected. There was nothing defiant about it, rather a humble and modest memorial of haunting beauty. Small tributes had been laid at the foot of the column. Flowers, scraps of poetry, ribbons, personal offerings left by those who had been here before her. A pair of tiny knitted blue boots for a baby.

Claire crouched down and picked them up. Blue for a boy. She wished she had thought to bring something of sentimental value to mark her passing. A photograph, perhaps. Too late now.

Resisting an urge to cross herself – she knew Cathars rejected such gestures – Claire stood up. Here, she felt the presence of the past all around her, benign ghosts who understood her purpose and had come to keep her company on her journey. In her mind's eye, she could see images of the women who had stood here before her, who had lived and loved and died in the protective embrace of the mountain.

She followed the path over the grass, then into the woods at the bottom of the mountain, climbing up through the box and evergreen, following a narrow track covered in ice and fallen leaves and the last vestiges of winter. Everything was silent, quiet.

Peaceful.

As the path turned a hairpin, Claire suddenly was out in the open, above the tree line. Now, she could see the road far below, snaking through the winter landscape, and ahead, the great white wall of the Pyrenees that divided France from Spain.

The higher she climbed, the more history came rushing back and pushed out her own, small memories. Claire imagined how those medieval pilgrims might have felt looking down from the citadel after ten months of siege to see the standards and banners of the Catholic Church and the fleur-de-lis of the French King flying below. In the castle, a hundred defenders. In the valley, between six and ten thousand men. An unequal fight. She thought of the mothers and fathers choosing to die in their faith, surrendering their children to be cared for by others before walking into the flames.

Higher into the clearer air, leaving the world far behind. Now Claire could picture the enemy mercenaries scaling the vertiginous slope on the south-eastern side of the mountain, attempting to take possession of the *Roc de la Tour*, a spike of stone rising up on the easternmost point of the summit ridge. Catapult and mangonel, an endless bombardment. For those trapped in the citadel, the relentless noise of the missiles must have broken their spirit as surely as they battered the castle walls.

Higher still and higher, up through the clouds.

Claire was only a few dozen yards from the main entrance. Her breath tore in her chest and her red duffel coat felt cumbersome, but she kept going, head down, until finally she reached the Great Gate.

Having planned this journey for so long, now she was finally here, she was suddenly reluctant to break the spell and enter. She needed to savour the moment. She feared the voices would be too strong. Or, perhaps worse, that she would not hear them at all. She took one last look out across the Ariège spread out below her, a patchwork of bare fields and evergreen firs, and then she stepped through the low, wide arch and into the ruins of the castle.

It was all much smaller and more confined than she'd expected, longer and thinner too. There was no beauty here, no mystery, just an empty shell of stone and rock. Claire stood in the uninhabited space. She had hoped to feel an immediate sense of homecoming, proof that she had made the right decision, but she felt nothing. An absence of emotion, neither good nor bad. And though she'd passed no one on the path going up or coming down, she was nonetheless surprised to find herself alone. She had thought the anniversary of the fall of Montségur might have drawn others, pilgrims like her, in search of the spirit of the past.

Claire looked around to get her bearings. Immediately opposite the Great Gate was another smaller arch, more like a door than a gate, which hundreds of years ago she knew had led down to the medieval village. Slowly, she began to walk around, examining the walls as if she could see pictures in the rocks. She went first to the western tip, where the main hall had been, peering, looking for significance, for meaning, in the stone and finding none. She persisted, walking now along the northern wall until she came to a crumbling staircase that had clearly once linked the lower to the upper floors of the keep. When she tilted her head and looked up, she could see the holes in the rock walls where perhaps the joists had rested.

Only then did Claire see she was not, in fact, the only visitor.

Someone was standing on the very top of the outer wall of the citadel, looking out over the valley. It was hard to be certain, but it looked like a woman. She narrowed her eyes. A woman with black hair in a long red coat that reached almost to the ground.

Claire took a step closer, wondering how she'd failed to notice her before and how she had managed to get up to that section of the wall. There were so many broken steps. The lower flight presented no problems, but then it simply stopped. It was as if two different workmen, one starting at the top, one at the bottom, had failed to meet. She wanted to call out, but it seemed intrusive and she didn't want to startle her fellow pilgrim. Even from this distance, Claire could see the top of the wall was narrow and it would be icy.

At the same time, she felt a fierce need to talk to her. She stepped up to the wall and ran her fingers over the handholds, looking for gaps in the stone, testing her weight. The woman's outline was clearer now, silhouetted against the cold, bright sky. She was about the same height and build as Claire, although her clothes were oddly old-fashioned. A moss-green dress hung beneath the hem of the red cloak, not a coat at all. She had now pulled the hood over her head, obscuring her face. Even so, there was something familiar about her stillness, her patience, as if she was keeping vigil high on the ancient walls. As if she was waiting for something or someone.

Claire began to climb.

She thought she could hear singing. The harsh sound of male voices this time, not the sweeter tones of women.

Veni, veni.

Claire pushed her fingers into crevices, forced her unwieldy boots into cracks in the rock, and pulled herself up. She did not fall.

Luck, determination, something carried her over the gap that yawned between the lower and upper levels, until, finally, she too was standing on the wall.

Claire took a step towards the woman.

'I'm here,' she said. 'I've come.'

The woman was standing on the very edge of the wall, even though she didn't seem to have moved. The edge of her dress skimmed the frosted ground. Claire sensed, rather than saw, she was smiling.

'At last,' the woman murmured as she stretched out a thin, white hand. '*A la perfin.*'

Claire took it. Together, they stepped out into the sky.

As they fell, the woman's hood fell back from her face. Claire smiled at the sight of familiar features looking back at her. Was it her ancestor, long dead or, rather, her old self, eyes bright and singing with hope, the person she had been before grief took the life from her?

Claire was home. No more past or future now, only an everlasting present.

*

The hire car was found a few days later, half buried in the snow. No one understood how she'd managed to reach the village in the first place. The blizzard had been one of the most sudden and the worst in living memory, shutting all roads in and out of the village from late on the evening of 15th March until early on the 19th.

Claire's body was never found, though they searched for weeks. After all, she had no further need of it.

Her diary, however, was discovered beneath a table in a local restaurant, lying open on the page for Friday 16th March. Since the owner and his wife had been away all winter, no one could explain how it came to be there. Not a suicide note, but the signs were all there. The unexplained death of her baby son in his cot: the not-knowing-why and the loss. The guilt. It was a grief that would never leave her, a loneliness that would never let go.

There were only two words written on the page – MONS SALVATIONIS – but the date was ringed in red.

Author's Note

In 1989, we bought a tiny house in the shadow of the medieval city walls of Carcassonne in the south-west of France, a region known as the Languedoc. The area is the inspiration for my trilogy of novels – *Labyrinth*, *Sepulchre* and *Citadel* – as well as various stories and essays.

This is one of the earliest stories I published. Written during 2003, the inspiration was my first visit to Montségur in the Pyrenees in the 1990s. My husband, two-year-old daughter and I left Carcassonne in a blaze of spring sunshine, yet found ourselves in the mountains in the grip of a blizzard.

We found a seemingly deserted restaurant, though there was a burning fire and food laid out on tables. In real life, of course, the owner had popped out and came back soon enough, but for some time we were the only people there.

In a story, things are different . . .

The title comes from the practice of illuminating manu-scripts where significant or important days are picked out in red, known as rubrics. The first Council of Nicaea in 325 CE decreed which were to be Saints' Days, Feasts and other Holy Days, which came to be printed on medieval church calendars in red. The term – a 'red letter day' – came into wider usage with the publication of the first Book of Common Prayer in 1549, in which the calendar showed special holy days illustrated in red ink.

The story was first published in an anthology called *Little Black Dress* edited by Susie Maguire.

THE DROWNED VILLAGE

The Quibéron Peninsula, Brittany
November 1912

The Drowned Village

The sea has many voices,
Many gods and many voices

from 'The Dry Salvages', *Four Quartets*
T. S. ELIOT

It was mid-November. Autumn was already stripping the trees, though winter had not taken a grip on the land. Farms and market gardens were still laden with fruit and vegetables. The seas were calm enough for even the most careful fisherman to put out on the tide.

In school it was the week allotted for the award of scholarships. Only once or twice in living memory had a child from the Three Villages gained a bursary to go and study at the secondary school in the city nearly twenty miles away.

Gaston made his way to the front of the hall. The teachers lined each wall, all eyes upon him, as he climbed the three steps onto the stage. Choked by nerves, he could barely raise his head.

The headteacher spoke. 'This day, the twenty-second of November 1912, is a very proud day for the Three Villages and our school.'

There was an immediate round of applause. It was Mme Martin who began it, Gaston was sure. She was his favourite teacher, strict without being unkind, keen on nature and science though she taught literature, considered and fair.

The headteacher held up his hands for quiet.

'Gaston, I believe you have something to say.'

Gaston looked round at the sea of faces. Children from the age of four up to his own classmates, eleven years old, at the top of the school. With the teachers, about sixty people waiting for him to say something important. He hesitated. All he could think about was his clothes – the shabby trousers with the let-down hems and his father's patched summer jacket, far too big but the only garment his mother said would do for a day such as this.

Then, at the back of the hall, there was a commotion. All heads turned and, to his mortification, Gaston saw his mother and father tottering in and trying to slip into the back row of chairs. His mother was trying to put on powder even though she had her arm threaded through her husband's, and her headscarf was crooked. They were both flushed, eyes a little too bright, in the way Gaston recognised and hated.

He could think of nothing to say.

Mme Martin firmly turned back to the stage and raised her hand. 'We are all very proud of you, Gaston.'

Gaston gave a small smile. 'Thank you,' he whispered.

She quickly moved to help get Gaston's parents seated. Silence surged through the hall. To Gaston each second lasted for ever, but though they fussed and were clumsy, finally they were seated and looking at the stage too.

'Gaston,' said the headteacher. 'You have something to say?'

Gaston remembered the piece of paper – Mme Martin had

suggested he should write something down rather than rely on memory – and quickly pulled it from the pocket of his hand-me-down trousers.

'I am very grateful to everyone. My teachers helped me to study and, because of that, I was able to win this scholarship. I will do my best to make everyone in the Three Villages proud.'

He bit his bottom lip, folded the piece of paper and twisted it in his fingers.

'Well done,' said the headteacher, leading the round of applause.

Gaston returned to his seat, trying not to catch his mother's eye. There were more prizes for each of the classes and a special gift for Mme Denis who was going to live with her sister in Quibéron.

When the ceremony was over, everyone lingered in the hall and Gaston had to endure the adults coming to congratulate him. He never knew what to say, so he smiled and nodded and mouthed thank you over and again. The men shook his hand or clapped him on the back. The women hugged him and said how he was growing.

Finally, he realised that the only people he hadn't seen were his own parents.

'They left,' said Régis. 'They asked Maman if you could come home with me. Said they'd fetch you later.'

'Oh.'

Gaston wasn't sure if he was disappointed or relieved. It was nothing new, but he thought today might be different.

'Oh,' he said again. 'All right.'

*

The journey to Régis's farm took a little over an hour in an old-fashioned trap pulled by two farm horses.

The boys sat on the second bench, behind Régis's parents. Monsieur and Mme Hélias were talking in low voices and the hooves of the horses and the clinker rattled loud in the crisp November air. Even so, Gaston caught some of the conversation, fragments about a ceremony due to take place tomorrow in which Régis's father, he gathered, had an important part to play.

He glanced at Régis.

'The Feast of St Colomban,' Régis whispered.

Gaston hadn't heard of it, but he nodded all the same. 'Are you going?'

'Not until I'm fourteen, though Papa says I can help with the bonfire tomorrow night.'

'Régis,' his father said sharply. 'Enough.'

'I wasn't saying anything out of turn, I was just . . .'

Monsieur Hélias glanced over his shoulder at Gaston. 'It is not for everyone.'

Gaston flushed. He knew what people thought of his family, how they tattled about them.

Régis's mother put her hand on her husband's arm.

'Joseph,' she murmured.

From the set of his shoulders, Gaston realised Régis's father was still angry, but he said nothing more. He clicked the reins and the trap jerked forward. Régis looked sideways at Gaston and shrugged, as if to apologise.

The rest of the journey passed in silence.

*

Gaston's parents didn't come.

After waiting up until nine o'clock, Monsieur and Mme Hélias finally went to bed, leaving the boys sitting by the fire and telling them not to be too late. The only sound was the ticking of the kitchen clock and the floorboards creaking upstairs. As soon as the house was quiet, Régis put down his book and gestured for Gaston to follow him.

'Come on,' he said in a whisper. 'I'll show you.'

'But if my . . .'

He stopped, the look on his friend's face making it clear Régis no more expected his father to show up now than he himself did.

'But what if your parents wake up and find we're not here?' he said instead.

'They won't. They're both up so early for the cows, they sleep like logs. Come on.'

*

The cold pinched at their cheeks as the boys made their way across the fields to the rocky gully that ran down to the beach of St Colomban.

The ground was damp, but they perched on the rocks beside the narrow stream for a while, without speaking. Listening to the sea rolling in between the headlands.

Then, suddenly, Régis's head snapped up. He turned to Gaston, his eyes bright in the dark, his voice brimming with excitement.

'There,' he said. 'Can you hear them?'

Gaston frowned. 'Who do you mean?'

'Them,' Régis said, dropping his voice. 'The dead who live beneath the sea.'

'You can't believe . . .' he began, then stopped. Gaston could see his friend was serious; this wasn't an old Halloween story.

Aware of Régis watching, he leaned forward and listened more intently. This time, above the slide and drag of the shingle, he could hear a low moaning sound. In the wind through the rocks, sculpted and pierced by countless tides, shrill voices, plaintive and lost. The nerves he'd felt standing in front of the whole school earlier came back, a sharp tug in the pit of his stomach.

'What's that noise?' he whispered.

'Did your parents never tell you the story?'

Gaston shook his head. They had, in truth, taught him next to nothing.

'Many thousands of years ago, or so it's said, there was a causeway there that led to an island. With every generation, with every high tide, it was eaten away little by little until, finally, there were only a few inhabitants left. They refused to go, though everyone here begged them to leave. Finally, when the highest of the spring tides came, the village was flooded and the island disappeared beneath the waves.'

Gaston stared, not sure what he was supposed to say.

'That's why there is a light beneath the water,' Régis continued in the same, low voice. 'They keep it burning for the drowned souls who live there. They eat limpets and blue mussels and seaweed and live in the caves with giant crabs. Fish swim around their heads and through their ribcages in great silver shoals.'

Gaston wanted to laugh, but the sound caught in his throat. He looked out to sea.

'I can't see a light,' he said.

'Over the year, it fades and goes out. That's what happens to-morrow on the Feast of St Colomban: they light it once more so the drowned village can been seen.'

For a moment, Gaston was silent. 'Your parents believe this old fisherwife's tale?'

'They talk about it when they think I'm not listening. It's true.' He paused. 'I believe it too.'

The boys fell silent, locked in their own thoughts. Gaston gazed out over the sea, pretending he wasn't looking for the glow of a lamp beneath the waves. He felt Régis had shared something important with him – even though it was a fairytale – and felt he ought to give something in return.

Gaston considered showing Régis the cave he'd discovered and the special things he had hidden there. Before he could suggest it, his friend was on his feet.

'Come on,' said Régis, 'I'm cold. Let's go back.'

Back in the farmhouse kitchen, the boys warmed themselves by the embers of the fire, eating bowls of rice pudding, then went to bed. When he slept, Gaston's dreams were filled with creatures of the sea, blue and green and transparent white. The image of a single lamp fading beneath the waves.

*

Despite the awards ceremony the day before, there was school on Saturday morning as usual.

Régis seemed to have caught a chill. His face looked damp and slightly flushed. His mother kept rushing in and out, busy with the butter churns, and paid the boys little attention. Gaston felt uncomfortable, though. Monsieur Hélias hadn't addressed a single word to him. He felt he was there on sufferance and when Monsieur Hélias did break his silence, it was to ask him whether his father was working today. Gaston felt even more certain he had outstayed his welcome.

The boys set off alone. Swaddled in rugs and scarves, Régis took the reins with a single horse harnessed in the trap. Once they were out of sight of the farmhouse, he threw off some of the woollens and drove on at a good lick. The trap clattered on the rutted path, bouncing and swinging towards the school.

From a distance, Gaston could see Mme Martin was standing at the gate and before they had even climbed down from the trap, she had beckoned for him to follow her.

He assumed it was something to do with the scholarship again, or more information about how it would be to be living away from home in a boarding school or about having to buy new books and pens, but she walked in silence down the corridor and her face was solemn.

She led him into an empty classroom and closed the door. 'Sit down, Gaston,' she said.

Quietly and gently, she told him that there had been an accident last night. His parents had both been killed outright. Their trap had come off the road and plunged down the bank into the old dew pond. Gaston knew neither of his parents could swim. No one knew why it had happened, she said, only that it had and he would have to be brave. There was nothing one can do except try to be strong and trust in providence. Could Gaston do that?

He heard the words, but could make no sense of them. He looked up into Mme Martin's worried, sympathetic face, then asked her to say it again. She put her hand on his shoulder.

Arrangements were being made, she reassured him. He wasn't to worry about any of the practical things.

'Would you like to be on your own?' she asked. 'The headmaster will allow you to sit in his office.'

Gaston shook his head. He would be all right.

'I'm so sorry,' she said. Mme Martin hesitated, then opened the door and he followed her back out into the corridor.

When he went into the playground, it was clear that the other children already knew. Régis was nowhere to be seen, so Gaston stood alone beneath the solitary *pin parasol* rolling a stone back and forth with his boot. When the bell rang and the school day began, he heard a girl in the class below talking about the accident and, unmistakably, the word 'drunk'.

Everyone fell silent as he walked past.

*

Mme Martin was attentive. Watchful. He noticed she kept looking at him, during the lesson, to see if he was bearing up.

At the end of the morning, while the other children were filing out to go home, he stopped at her desk.

'What should I do, Madame? Should I go home?'

Mme Martin shook her head. 'I think the headmaster wants you to stay here until arrangements had been made. I'll see if I can't find out.'

Remembering the whispering of the girls, the way everyone stopped talking, he was grateful to be allowed to stay inside.

Gaston lost himself in an adventure story by Jules Verne. He was surprised when one of the little children came by to announce the end of school, clanging the big handbell clutched in two small fists.

As the other children picked up their coats and put on their outdoor shoes, Mme Martin gestured to Gaston to stay where he was. He stood by the window into the yard and watched the other children separating and heading home. Then the playground was empty and the caretaker appeared with his rake and his wheelbarrow to tidy up the fallen leaves.

'This evening, Monsieur and Madame Hélias have very kindly said you may stay another night with them. On Sunday we will speak to the curate and he will organise something. I understand you have no other relations.'

'No.'

Mme Martin sighed. She shook her head and, for a moment, Gaston thought she was going to say something else of importance, but she didn't.

'I am so very sorry,' she said. 'But we will work something out in the end, I'm sure of it.'

'Yes.'

'Yes,' she echoed. 'Well, until Monday.'

Régis's horse was in the stable yard at the back of the tiny school. They hitched the trap, said goodbye to the caretaker and set out along the rough path back to the farm.

They didn't say much. Régis was clearly tongue-tied, not sure what to say, and besides his cold was worse. It suited Gaston. In truth, he was numb. The news hadn't really sunk in. Or perhaps it had, but he couldn't really believe it. He hadn't cried. He didn't know if he was sad or just frightened about what was going to happen to him. As the cart bumped along, Gaston thought about all the times he'd sat on the smooth stone at the end of the path to his house, waiting for his parents to come home. Sometimes he sat out in the rain, craning for a glimpse of them on the narrow road, not knowing if they would come at all and dreading the smell of the bar on their breath and clothes, but hoping all the same.

Régis stopped the trap, pulling gently back on the reins. A sheep had strayed onto the path.

'Could you get that animal out of the way? I'm not feeling very well.'

Gaston bit his lip. 'Do you remember when I was the smallest boy in class?'

Régis rubbed his nose on his sleeve. 'What?'

'Even the girls were taller than me. They called me Little Gaston. Remember?'

Régis coughed. 'I didn't know you then. Look, I really don't feel so good. The sooner you get that sheep out of the way, the sooner we'll be home.'

With a spurt of irritation at the self-pity in his friend's voice – he was the one who deserved sympathy, not Régis and another of his spluttering colds – Gaston jumped down from the cart. He chased the sheep out of the way, then looked up at his friend.

'Come on then,' said Régis, 'let's get back.'

Gaston shook his head. The breeze made the frayed bottoms of his trousers flap about his ankles.

'You go. I don't want to talk to anybody.'

'I'll get into trouble.'

'I'll only be in the way. They'll be pleased I'm not with you.'

'I can't leave you. Mme Martin said.'

Gaston shrugged. 'Tell them I made you. You couldn't stop me.'

The two boys stared at each other, then Régis nodded.

'All right,' he said. After a pause, he added: 'I'm sorry. I mean, I know they weren't . . . well, they were still your parents.'

'Yes.'

'Don't be long.'

'I won't. You go.'

Régis clicked his tongue and slapped the reins across the horse's flank, then the axles rumbled as the trap pulled away into the November afternoon.

Gaston waited until his friend was out of sight, then struck out across the fields and along the coast to where the gulley ran down to the beach. When he drew close, he saw bundles of hazel twigs set ready for the Festival of St Colomban that night. He didn't care about that. He just wanted somewhere to sit on his own for an hour or two. He carefully picked his way down towards a place in the rocks where a shallow cave had eaten into the cliff face. He went as deep into the calm gloom as he could and sat very still, his knees drawn up to his chest and his arms around his knees. Outside, the drizzle began to fall and the sky was stormy. Gaston's eyes clouded over and he wondered how different life would be now he was completely alone.

*

When Gaston awoke, at first he had no idea where he was. He was lying on his side, using his right arm for a pillow. It was dark now, but he realised he wasn't particularly cold.

He yawned, stretched, then realised he was hungry. He hoped there would be a good dinner at Régis's house. Then, he remembered. First, about his parents and the accident. Then, coming hard on its heels, that tonight it was the Feast of St Colomban so there would more than likely be no supper.

Gaston felt with his hands across the floor of the cave. He

found the niche in the wall – a natural rupture in the rock – where he had secreted a few special things: the skull of a pheasant picked clean by birds and insects, a bone so big that it must have come from the carcass of some great whale. He knew them by touch and they comforted him. There was also a beautifully built nest containing three speckled eggs from the cliff. It was Régis who'd persuaded Gaston to climb down the cliff face and steal them, even though the curate had visited their classroom to explain that the roosts were protected by law and should not be disturbed.

Outside the cave, Gaston could now hear the waves and the wind beginning their night-time complaint. The sound, echoing gently about him in the cave, sounding more like human voices now. He rubbed his hands across his face. It reminded him of how his grandfather used to stroke his brow with his hard fisherman's hands, dried out by salt and wind. They had been happy then. But then he died and his parents, rather than living as they had before, spent the inheritance on drink and visits to the town. Gaston imagined his own hands hardened by toil and wondered if the same thing would happen to his heart.

A trick of the tide brought a wave crashing in through the entrance to the cave. The water seemed iridescent, bringing light into the hollow, illuminating the rock like a wavering white flame. Gaston sprang to his feet, suddenly frightened. He tucked his shirt into his trousers, doing up his father's patched summer jacket to the throat, placed his treasures back in the niche in the rock and went outside. He didn't want to be trapped by the tide. He didn't want to put anybody out and he didn't want Régis to be in trouble for not having taken care of him.

The sight that awaited him drove all domestic thoughts from his mind. The sea seemed turned to glass, smooth as a millpond without a ruck or ripple on its surface. Even the edge of the surf was still, like a wavering line drawn in chalk across the wet sand. The air was tense and still with no sound of wind.

He had never known the sea to behave in this way.

There was a noise from the path above. Gaston stepped back into the shadows and stared up. He saw a line of men and women, all adults, walking in silent and single file down the gulley towards the beach. In the strange, flat light of the glistening surface of the sea, he saw each carried one of the tight bundles of hazel under their arms.

As he watched, they stacked them in a pile, twice the height of a man, and then formed a semicircle behind it, facing the shore. There were perhaps twenty-five of them, each wrapped in dark cloaks with deep hoods.

Then, as if there had been some signal, the water began to break and to shudder. Gaston peered out into the flickering darkness and saw the sea was now starting to shift and slip and slide. Something was emerging from the waves, a human form walking slowly but purposefully up onto the beach. The shape – it was impossible to tell whether man or woman – was wrapped in a cloak that seemed to be woven entirely from dancing ribbons of flame.

As the first figure broke through the shallows, another followed, then another, each trailing seaweed from their ankles. They dripped with brine that hissed and spat and billowed up about their faces in a mask of steam. And still they came, all striding with the same steady, purposeful gait, until some fifty or sixty of them were standing on the beach, treading from foot to foot, marching on the spot, turning this way and that.

They began to murmur, their plaintive sound an echo of the sea and the wind on the shingle, their voices growing louder and louder.

He glanced at those who had lit the bonfire on the far side of the semicircle, not sure if they too could see these ancient inhabitants of the drowned village or if he was the only one.

He knew he should remain hidden, but he could not help himself. He felt drawn to them. The unexpected movement attracted their attention. Six or seven of the drowned figures turned towards him. At first, they were still. Then they were floating across the sand, holding out their hands. Gaston stepped back. They smelt like last week's catch trampled in the bottom of the boat. They smelt of death, and yet Gaston was still drawn. He could feel the warmth of the flames that seemed to engulf them. Then thin fingers were gripping his wrists and his elbows and his neck and pulling him in to the heart of the throng.

Gaston knew that he should be terrified, but instead he felt welcomed, weightless and supported, as the creatures carried him up the beach to the bonfire. Immediately, all movement ceased. Gaston hung suspended between two worlds. He could move neither forward nor back. And he somehow knew that the visitors from beneath the sea were waiting for some kind of signal.

Could the villagers see him? Could they see the ghost women and men who had come, warmed by the light of the bonfire?

The first chime of midnight sounded. Gaston's sense of calm started to desert him. The wailing started to build in volume once more as six of the drowned hauled their flaming cloaks from their shoulders and threw them onto the stack of burning hazel. Immediately, they caught and sent sparks of white and green shooting through the flames. A second chime, and others stepped forward: twelve of the creatures, seeming to shudder and tremble with the memory of the moment at which the waves closed over their head.

A third and a fourth and a fifth chime brought the same result. Gaston was frightened now. He flinched at the rattle of limpet-encrusted bones as, one by one, the visitors relinquished their cloaks. They shivered, draped in a few shreds of flesh, turning their awful faces left and right before the flames.

The church bell rang out again across the coastline. Gaston felt himself drawn forward, this time towards two children. As thin as he was, he knew he was not one of them and wanted to pull away, yet he found himself powerless to resist. The waifs clutched at him with skeletal hands, dragging the jacket from his shoulders, their tragic voices high and shrill like the desperate wind.

Gaston tried to cry out, but his voice was swamped by the voices of the drowned. Why was no one helping him? Why were the villagers standing by and allowing this to happen? He heard the tenth strike of the bell. Now the children were pulling at the buttons on his thin shirt, desperate to consign everything to the pyre before the final stroke of midnight.

'Help me,' Gaston called out, finding his voice at last. 'They will take me. They want to take me with them.'

He tried to wriggle free, but the children's hands were clamped fast around his ankles, his wrists.

The eleventh chime.

'Help me please.'

At the very last moment, Gaston managed to shake himself

free and leap back out of their reach. The children, cheated of their prize, threw off their cloaks and cast them onto the bonfire. It was now burning twenty feet into the air. The sparks danced against the night and the final stroke sounded.

The final toll of the bell.

Immediately, silence. Immediately, the ghostly congregation fell still. None of them, now, paid any attention to Gaston. They were as transfixed by the fire as he had been transfixed by their apparition.

Gaston realised that he could hear the surf once more. The sea was in motion, a gentle swell sending shallow waves up onto the sand. Normal for this time of year. The flames were diminishing. The magical garments of fire had almost consumed the stack of hazel bundles.

Then, the villagers on the far side of the flames drew back the hoods of their dark cloaks. Gaston gasped, recognising Régis's mother and Monsieur Hélias too, standing to one side of the semicircle. As the bonfire burned down, Gaston saw the curate and, standing to his left, Mme Martin. None of them seemed to be able to see him, though. At least, they gave no sign of it.

One of the drowned stepped forward. A man with broad shoulders, though he was all bone and seaweed now. He paused and then bowed low to the living. The curate answered his gesture. The dead man leant forward and plucked a white-hot ember from the ashes, then turned to face the sea.

He held the ember aloft, as if in triumph, then he began to pace purposefully, steadily back down the beach towards their drowned village. The others fell into step behind him.

Gaston watched them go. Some of them seemed to hesitate before treading reluctantly into the surf. One after another they disappeared beneath the black waves until finally only the two children were left. They paused for a moment and turned back, whether towards the fire and its warmth or to invite Gaston to come with them, he could not say.

Then a few steps more and they were gone.

All at once, without his jacket and shirt, with the fire burned down to ashes, Gaston fell to his knees and sobbed, the tears running down his face and over his hands. Crying for those condemned to come ashore once a year to light their kingdom under the sea, crying for the grief and loneliness inside him that drew him to their company. Crying for his parents.

Then, the warmth of real arms around him and he was being pulled to his feet. The sound of a familiar voice.

'Gaston, how do you come to be here?'

It was Mme Martin's voice.

'I didn't mean to . . .' he tried to explain. 'I fell asleep. I didn't know, I didn't mean to spy.'

He felt a cloak being wrapped around his shaking shoulders.

'You're safe now, don't worry. Everything will be all right.'

She walked him up the beach. 'Everything will be all right.'

*

Monsieur Hélias picked him up in the trap, promising that Régis was back at the farmhouse and there would be a good meal waiting. He didn't seem angry now and Gaston thought, perhaps, he had misjudged the man. As they rounded the headland, he turned in his seat.

'Look,' he said.

Some two hundred yards out at sea, where once the island had been, a light was burning. The drowned islanders had relit their warning lamp from the embers of the bonfire.

Mme Martin smiled. 'Yes.'

'But how is it possible?' he said. 'How can it burn beneath the waves?'

'How is any of it possible?' she laughed. 'Perhaps it's just a trick of the light.'

'Even so,' he said quietly. 'I saw it. It must be true, somehow, mustn't it?'

'Who's to say?' she said. 'We must trust to providence.'

'What does it mean?' he said, his voice little more than a whisper.

'Perhaps only that we have to believe that the future can be different from the past.' She paused. 'I have been very proud to teach you, Gaston. I believe that you will give us all reason to be proud when you go away to boarding school.'

'I can still go? I feared . . . I thought maybe not.'

'The scholarship will pay your expenses and your parents' money will be set aside for when you leave, for when you are a man. Your writing impressed the Board very much.'

'And then what will I do?'

'I don't know,' said Mme Martin, but he could hear the smile in her voice. 'Perhaps you will write a book about the legends of the Quibéron Peninsula. Set this story down.'

Gaston took a last look at the lamp burning out at sea, then turned back to face her.

'Perhaps I will,' he said.

Author's Note

My lovely Uncle Geoff died in February 2011. A passionate musician and a Francophile, he was a great favourite at Christmas get-togethers with his stories of visits to festivals, food and music, all over France. The year when he fell asleep – properly asleep – on the floor under the Christmas tree, has gone down in family history. When my inspirational Auntie Margie* died last year, and their house came to be cleared, my cousins suggested I might like some of Uncle Geoff's French books.

Three boxes were duly delivered. They contained, as well as notebooks and clippings from newspapers, a wonderful mixture of novels, cookbooks, art and illustrated guidebooks. But the biggest treasures were several volumes of Breton folk tales and legends. Some stories were similar to myths I'd heard from Cornwall or Wales, even Sussex, but most were new to me and came very specifically from the coastline and landscape of Brittany past and present.

---

* The Reverend Margaret Booker was one of the founders of the Movement for the Ordination of Women. She was ordained by the Bishop of Chelmsford on 30th April 1994, the first woman to be ordained in that Diocese.

'The Drowned Village' is the first of two stories inspired by those Breton folk tales and is dedicated to the memory of my uncle and aunt.

THE HOUSE ON THE HILL

Dean Hall, West Sussex

October 1922

The House on the Hill

All houses wherein men have lived and died
Are haunted houses. Through the open doors
The harmless phantoms on their errands glide,
With feet that make no sound upon the floors.

from 'Haunted Houses'
HENRY WADSWORTH LONGFELLOW

In the house on the hill, there was a light. A single, flickering flame in a room on the first floor, like a candle burning.

Daphne looked at it from her bedroom in Dean Hall, her hands resting on the cold stone window sill. Her train from London had been late getting in, so she'd barely had time to say her hello to her cousin, Teddy, before being shown to her room. The other weekend guests had arrived some time before. She hadn't had the chance to explore the parkland and was surprised there was so substantial a house within the grounds. It looked both rather splendid and rather isolated, despite its proximity to Dean Hall. Set on the ridge of the hill between two clusters of trees, a façade of brick, perfectly symmetrical, red tiled roof and tall chimneys. Though half hidden in the shadows of the woods,

Daphne imagined there'd be a fine view from the house across the South Downs and down to the sea some eight miles away. She wondered if Teddy knew who lived there or if the house even belonged to the estate. He had taken Dean Hall on a six month lease and this was the first of his weekend house parties. She doubted he knew much about the place yet, though he'd sent her a photograph from the letting agent.

In the dying light, Daphne could make out the silhouette of the arboretum higher up the wooded hillside. Spread out below that, she knew, were fields of yellow rape like squares of a patchwork quilt, furrowed and brown now in the autumn.

She shivered, feeling the chill air creep over her bare skin, and drew back inside the comfort of her room. Daphne pulled the window closed, stiff on its mullioned hinges, and rattled at the metal catch until it was properly shut. She lingered at the window a moment longer, her gaze fixed upon the flickering orange of light on the distant hill, mesmerised, until suddenly it was gone.

If she'd been a jumpy kind of girl, she might have squealed. As it was, Daphne felt oddly put out, as if someone had caught her snooping and blown the candle out. She pulled more roughly at the curtains than she'd intended to block out the encroaching autumn night. The brass rings rattled on the rails, but didn't want to shift. She gave it up as a bad job and left them for the maid. At Dean Hall, Teddy had stressed in his letter inviting her for the weekend, there was still staff to keep things ticking over. Like in the old days, before the war, when everything was easier.

The old days.

If Douglas hadn't deserted her, life would have been so different.

As Daphne started to dress for dinner, she thought of her temporary room in the boarding house in Berwick Street, the single gas ring in the kitchen shared by four girls like her, who had not been brought up to earn a living by typing or working in a shop. She thought of the tatty WC at the end of the corridor, and nylon stockings hanging over the bath, the scarcity of hot water, and could have cried for the world she had left behind. Mrs Daphne Dumsilde, it had such a ring to it. Douglas had promised to look after her, in sickness and in health.

But he had not looked after her. He hadn't kept his word.

Daphne folded her travelling clothes on the armchair and shimmied into a silk underslip, appalled at how easily she had immediately fallen back into her habitual blue state of mind. Why spoil a perfectly pleasant weekend? Invitations had been thin on the ground – a woman alone was always awkward and her circumstances made it doubly so – and she was too proud to ask for help. At Dean Hall there would be plenty of hot water, plenty of food and drink, perhaps a little dancing and amusing company to keep the dark thoughts at bay. She was glad to be here. Her cousin had seen out the war in America and had been abroad when the business with Douglas happened – but she liked Teddy and was determined not to spoil his weekend by being dull and gloomy.

In her slip and stockings, Daphne walked to the armoire and took a cigarette from her case, trying not to notice the inscription on the inside of the lid: To DeeDee from DeeDum, their little joke. She tapped it sharply to tighten the tobacco, picked up her Ronson and jabbed at it with her thumb until it sparked. That, too, reminded her of Douglas. How idiotic that she kept the case and lighter to remind her of happier times, when in fact the sight of them only made her feel worse.

Daphne inhaled, feeling the calming smoke seep down into her lungs. From the Oak Hall below, she heard the sound of the gramophone and whispers of jazz. Oddly modern music for so antique a setting. Madrigals and spinets would suit the wooden panels and trophies of big game hunts mounted on mahogany surrounds rather better than the smudged chords of Louisiana and New Orleans.

She glanced back to the window, wondering if there would be a light in the house on the hill again, but it was dark in the park. Night had fallen, stripping the shape and character from the pleasant Sussex landscape. Tomorrow morning, she promised herself, she would take a walk, perhaps sit a while and paint, aim for a likeness of the wonderful flint façade of Dean Hall. Or, rather, perhaps she would go in search of the house on the hill, and paint that instead. She felt strangely drawn to it.

Daphne stubbed out her cigarette and finished dressing for dinner. A soft pink silk dress, which suited her pale colouring, with a dropped handkerchief waist and low V beaded neckline. Peach stockings and a light woollen blue shawl, to cover her bare arms. A ribbon tied around her forehead, a mist of scent, and she was ready. Daphne hesitated a moment, then removed her wedding ring and left it on the table beside the bed. She didn't know if other guests would know about her situation but, whether they did or not, where was the sense in inviting questions?

Her bedroom was at the far corner of the south wing on the first floor. She stepped out into the dimly lit corridor, hearing sounds of the party down below, feeling a mixture of shyness and nerves at the thought of a roomful of strangers. She walked slowly, past perfectly acceptable paintings of sea and countryside, until she noticed, close to the top of the stairs, something delightful. A wonderful doll's house, painted façade of brick, perfectly symmetrical, red tiled roof and tall chimneys. In the gable there was a clock, showing the time set at three forty-five and the date: 1810. She ran her finger over the surface. There were ribbons of dust on the slope of the red roof and chimneys, but it was still charming. Daphne had owned a doll's house when she was little. It kept her entertained for hours, as she moved the tiny people from room to room, inventing lives for them, playing house. This doll's house was far grander and there was also something familiar about it. Daphne wondered if she'd perhaps seen a picture of it somewhere, it was so distinctive, but she couldn't bring anything to mind.

The noise from the Oak Hall was louder now and Daphne knew she should go down and join the party, but instead she unhooked the latch and opened it up to look inside.

The wooden façade swung open, revealing the entire household from top to bottom. A staircase ran like a spine up the middle of the house. At the lowest level were the working rooms – servants and a flock of geese and ducks, the mud room with harness, and the kitchen, with brass copper pots and an old rocking chair to one side. Cloth and wood figurines of a cook, parlour maids, and butler and boot boy, all perfectly dressed in black and white and green waistcoats. On the ground floor, a red and grey tiled entrance hall, a stone fireplace with marble mantel and a grandmother clock. To the left, a billiard room with the green baize table perfectly smooth and, to the right the dining room, with twelve mahogany chairs set round a polished oval table, and a maid in black and white uniform dusting the sideboard. On the floor above, the ladies and gentlemen of the house, whiskered and gowned in a drawing room and, above the billiard room, a study. A leather-topped desk, complete with inkwell and papers, bookshelves and a brass side table on which stood the smallest of glasses and a fold of paper, like a letter waiting to be read. Daphne frowned, something about this room in particular setting a memory scuttling in her mind. The chair was on its side. She reached in and picked it up, placing it back at the desk.

On the floors above, the family bedrooms. Each perfect in their detail, porcelain washbasins and jugs, matching counter-panes and portraits in tortoiseshell frames. In the attic, the maids' quarters and a nursery with a metal cot and blackboard and chalk.

The gong rang for dinner, its brass song reverberating up from the hall below. Knowing she couldn't put off joining the party any longer, Daphne reluctantly stood up and closed the glass fronted doors. She wondered if the doll's house had been modelled on a real house, if it had been made for the daughter of the family that once owned Dean Hall, or whether it was a recent acquisition for decoration only.

The gong sounded again.

Daphne straightened her dress and her stockings, and was about to rush down the stairs when she noticed a pinpoint of light in the miniature study. Uneven, like the light from a candle flickering in a draught. She looked along the corridor, assuming it had to be some kind of reflection from the wall lamps bouncing off the glass frontage of the doll's house, but the angles seemed wrong.

She cupped her hands over the glass and looked at the room on the first floor. Now, the study was dark again, of course it was, though the tiny chair was, once again, lying on its side. As if kicked away from the desk.

The final gong bellowed for dinner and, this time, Daphne heard Teddy shouting her name to hurry up. She ran to the minstrel's gallery and waved down to the assembled company. She hurried down the stairs, suppressing a shudder as she passed the ghastly floor-to-ceiling display of stuffed birds. The hard beaded eyes and frozen feathers of the robins and blackbirds and malevolent cranes stood motionless behind the glass.

*

Teddy knew nothing about another house on the estate – though he knew there were a few grace-and-favour cottages for farm workers – and nothing about any of the pieces of art dotted around the Hall.

He was, however, an excellent host and the evening passed in a haze of vermouth and ragtime. The company was congenial and Daphne flirted a little with a boy who worked in a dispensary, putting out of her mind, for a while, the drab existence to which she would have to return on Monday morning.

Later, while the men talked finance, she got into a conversation with a girl from Surrey about the best new detective novels. Like Daphne, she thought Poirot rather tiresome and preferred Mrs Sayers' Lord Peter Wimsey. An intimacy established, Daphne realised the girl was building up to ask about Douglas and everything came rushing back again, as it always did. Quickly, she excused herself and went in search of coffee. By the time she came back, the girl had moved on to someone else. It was, Daphne thought savagely, why she rarely ventured out. It was too dull always to have all eyes on her.

*

The party started to wind down at three o'clock in the morning. The men were slumped in the low armchairs with their ties loosened and their eyes bleary with booze and smoke. One of the girls had passed out on the sofa in the Oak Hall. Teddy had long since taken himself off to bed.

Daphne slipped away, averting her gaze from the display case as she climbed the stairs. The upstairs corridor was in shadow now and, though she glanced as she passed, there was no light to be seen in the doll's house.

Her room was cold, the meagre fire in the grate long since burnt out. The maid had turned down the bed, but omitted to close the curtains. The house on the hill was no longer visible, but out on the Downs, the glint of white chalk in the Sussex soil turned over by the plough glistened white in the moonlight, like fragments of bone.

Daphne undressed and got in to her wonderfully warm cotton pyjamas. Before, she would have worn a nightgown, regardless of the temperature, knowing her appearance at night mattered quite as much as her appearance during the day. Now, she could at least put comfort before glamour. In fact, she'd taken up many things since Douglas had gone. Smoking, drinking cocktails and wearing trousers. Without her husband at her side, she could at last please herself.

But as she climbed into the cold bed, even though she told herself the evening had been a roaring success and a welcome change from her usual scratch suppers eaten alone with just a magazine for company, the stark truth was that she still felt as lonely as she ever did.

*

Daphne wasn't sure what woke her, shortly after five in the morning. One moment she was fast asleep, dreaming of the beach at Deauville, the sun on her skin and sand between her toes and Douglas's arm resting on her shoulders. The next moment, she was wide awake, heart pounding and mouth dry.

She sat up, hearing nothing. The silence of the sleeping house surged around her, interrupted only by the gurgling of the water pipes, but yet there was something. As if the air itself was alive.

Daphne waited for her eyes to adjust, then realised it was a disturbance of light, not sound, that had roused her. Through the window, the sky was no longer black, but the colour of an August sunset. It took a moment to gather her wits, then she flung back the covers and ran to the glass. In the space between the two clusters of trees, where she had seen the single candle burning, the sky was now orange and gold. Fierce and violent flames, flickering and dancing.

The house on the hill was burning.

Daphne pushed her feet into her travelling shoes, pulled her coat over her pyjamas and, not bothering who might see her, ran out of her room. Down the corridor, shouting to raise the alarm even though she didn't know whether any other of the guests were in this part of the house. The blaze seemed to be inside almost, the orange glow reflecting off the glass surfaces, making it look as if the corridor itself, the doll's house itself, the petrified birds, were on fire too.

Down the main stairs, struggling with the bolts on the heavy front door, Daphne flew out into the night. Still shouting, assuming others would hear and follow. Somehow, she thought she might be able to help. The sky was overcast now, grey clouds – or smoke, she couldn't be sure – obscuring the face of the moon. She couldn't even see the house, hidden between the trees and the curve of the hill, but Daphne ran over the lawns and to the track she'd seen from her bedroom window.

She couldn't understand why no one else was out here. Surely the farm workers must have seen something. Her throat was raw from shouting and from the exertion of running. The muscles in her legs complained at the steep gradient of the hill, but Daphne forced herself on.

At last, she did catch a glimpse of someone. Some distance ahead of her, clearing the brow of the hill. She had no breath to call out – besides, she didn't want to slow him down – but she hoped he'd had more success than her in raising help.

Still she kept going, long strides, half stumbling, half running, keeping the man in her sights. One of Teddy's other guests? The closer she got, the more she felt sure she knew him – the cut of his jacket, his silhouette in the burning sky – and this time, she called out.

'Please! Wait.'

He either did not hear her, or heard her, but didn't stop.

Suddenly, between the trees, Daphne found herself in front of the house. For a split second, before she realised that everything was wrong, the only thought that went through her mind was how perfectly beautiful it was. The wooden painted façade and sloping red tiled roof and tall stack chimneys. The clock and the date: 1810. An exact copy of the doll's house on the first floor of the Hall, in fact. Of course, that was why it had seemed familiar earlier. She frowned. No, that was ridiculous. It was the other way round. This was the original, the child's toy the copy.

Then, a less welcome thought chasing hard on the heels of the other. The house was fine, utterly untouched, undamaged. How could that be?

Daphne felt a cold trickle run down her spine. There was no crackling of flames, no heat scorching the trees and her face, no sign that anything was wrong. The only sign of life was that one single flame, like a candle, shining in a room on the first floor.

She looked up and saw there was a peculiar translucent orange glow in the sky, behind the clouds, so she hadn't imagined that. Besides, the man had clearly seen something too. Like her, had come to help. But where was he?

'Hello?'

It didn't occur to her not to go in. She took a step towards the front door, then another. When she tried the handle, it swung open to reveal red and grey tiles on the floor and a staircase straight ahead.

'Is there anybody here?'

No one answered. She hesitated a moment more, then stepped into the entrance hall with its stone fireplace and marble mantel. She heard the ticking of the grandmother clock and, though there was no sign of him or anyone else, Daphne knew she wasn't alone.

'Where are you?'

Then, on the floor above, she heard a sound. A thud, like a piece of furniture falling over. And, in that moment between one beat of her heart and the next, she understood. Drawn inexorably now, Daphne went to the stairs and walked slowly up, heading towards the room on the first floor where that solitary flame still burnt.

At the top, she turned right and looked at the study door. It was ajar. Daphne carried on, one step further, another and another. Now the flat of her hand was on the wooden panel, pushing it wide open. Knowing – fearing – what she was going to see. A low armchair and brass table to her left, the folded letter there and the candle. Ahead, the chair kicked away from the desk. The photograph with her image in the tortoiseshell frame.

She could feel there was someone in the room with her. Slowly, she turned and saw the image that had haunted her for five years. Slowly, she raised her eyes and forced herself to see now, in this house on the hill, what she had never seen in life. Feet swinging in the air, hands limp and lifeless by his side, a man hanging, twisting in the still air.

'No . . .'

Daphne clamped her hand to her mouth to stop herself from screaming. She couldn't know whether he was a ghost or an imprint left in time, only that it was Douglas – her Douglas – just as he had been found, in the study of his parents' house, five years ago. Douglas, who had promised to look after her, but who had been unable to live with his nightmares of gas and barbed wire and his friends lying dead in the trenches. Leaving a letter saying he didn't want to be a burden, certain that she'd be better off without him, Douglas had left her to cope alone.

But now, as she forced herself to look on his beloved, lifeless face, she saw a kind of peace. Finally, Daphne understood. He had been unable to save himself, but he had saved her. She had blamed him for leaving her. Been angry with him. Now the time had come to grieve. She could miss him and mourn the loss of their shared life together, but then set her eyes to the future.

The tears began to fall.

*

They found her hours later, still dazed. Appearing, as Teddy put it later, like a wraith out of the mist. Cold, rather disorientated, but otherwise all right.

It turned out Daphne had been extremely lucky. There had been some kind of electrical short circuit in the south wing. The wiring in the top corridor had blown and the sparks had set fire to the doll's house and taken hold. The old summer curtains and brocade stored on the wooden slatted shelves in the housekeeper's room had caught next and burnt like paper and tinder, cutting off Daphne's room from the rest of the house. She wouldn't have stood a chance. She would have been overcome by smoke long before the fire had reached her.

The gardener had tried to get a ladder up to her window, but been beaten back by the flames. They'd called out and shouted, but when she hadn't answered, they'd feared the worst. It was only as dawn broke and Daphne appeared from the direction of the park, they realised she hadn't been in her room at all.

'What I don't understand,' Teddy had said, 'is what the hell you were doing out in the gardens in the middle of the night anyway.'

Daphne tried to explain how she had seen a light burning in the house on the hill, about the man she had followed away from the Hall, but Teddy shook his head. There was no other house on the estate – he had asked around – just workmen's cottages, certainly nothing grand. As for the doll's house, it had been bought by the current owners from a Belgian dealer. It wasn't connected with Dean Hall at all.

And then he patted her hand and, though everyone smiled and said how lucky she'd been, Daphne could see they thought she was in shock. That she was imagining things. The pity in their eyes burned her and she fell silent and turned away.

But Daphne knew. She knew, now, what had happened.

Later, as she rested on the sofa in the Oak Hall – having accepted Teddy's invitation to stay at Dean Hall as long as she liked, until she felt well enough to go back to London – Daphne began to plan. How she would leave Berwick Street and return to the little house in Chelsea she'd abandoned after Douglas's death.

Now it was up to her.

Next year, would be better. It was time to begin again.

Author's Note

This story was inspired by the West Dean Estate in Sussex, the former country home of Edward James. A great benefactor and patron of the arts – dance, sculpture and painting in particular – he was a significant supporter of the Surrealist artists; the original Dali lobster telephone and lips sofa started their life there. When James died, he left the house to be 'an Eden for the arts'. The flint-faced mansion is still at the heart of the college and filled with many of James's curios and oddities from his travels, from cases of stuffed birds to a giraffe's head. A magnificent five-storey doll's house, dating from the seventeenth century, is thought to be one of the oldest examples anywhere in the world.

A shorter version of the story was first published in *Woman & Home* magazine in 2009.

WHY THE YEW TREE
LIVES SO LONG

Kingley Vale, West Sussex
The Past & Present

Why the Yew Tree Lives So Long

The Lives of Three Wattles, The Life of a Hound;
The Lives of Three Hounds, The Life of a Steed;
The Lives of Three Steeds, The Life of a Man;
The Lives of Three Men; The Life of an Eagle;
The Lives of Three Eagles, The Life of a Yew,
The Lives of Three Yews, The Length of an Age.

TRADITIONAL

Once, the Yew tree lived and died in the company of its friends, the blackthorn and the hawthorn, the birch, the spindle, the ash and the oak. The Yew did not envy the blighted elm or the vulnerable hazel, with their passing brief lives, but it had no ambition to live longer than any other tree in the forest. It was content with its allotted time, by the way of things that were always and forever so.

Neolithic man cleared the wildwood of Kingley Vale for grazing animals and crops, but the Yew on the lower slopes did not mind. Later, Bronze Age artisans constructed burial mounds on the chalky grasslands and limestone hills above the woods, the sleeping tombs of warriors long dead. Later and later still, on the summit of Bow Hill, came the Devil's Humps and Goosehill Camp and a shabby temple to Roman Gods, and still the Yew did not object. As time walked its steady pace, beneath the dappled light and its ancient green shadow in the glade, Jutes and Britons and Angles breathed and lived and sighed and loved. These tribes were not the same, any more than the trees of the forest were the same. These tribes were not fashioned by the same rituals or traditions or superstitions, yet they lived side by side, in harmonious coexistence, as did the trees. Yew with birch with willow with conifer.

But then, then.

*

In the year 874 came the Vikings, came the Vikings who seized and burnt and destroyed. They swept north from Chichester into the Sussex weald and forest of Kingley Vale. The Saxon defenders sought sanctuary among the ancient green and mossy pathways where the Yew trees held sway, but found no respite there. The Yew could only watch and grieve as, day after night after day, the once silent groves echoed with the violence of sword and shield, shriek of iron and split bone. The inhumanity of it, the pointlessness of it, slipped weeping into the leaf and the bough of the Yew tree, turning the brown bark to purple. And the presentiment of death seeped into the berries, staining the pale, subtle fruit a vivid red.

Then the Yew understood that the cycle of things had changed. How their destiny was to stand witness, memorials to those who had fallen in order that such things should not happen again. That they must live until the lesson of harmony had been remembered. They did not wish it, they did not wish to be left behind as the rowan and the sycamore and the beech passed into different lives, different dimensions, but they accepted it was their lot because of the battles that had been fought beneath their branches. So where each warrior fell in Kingley Vale, a Yew touched the earth with long, trailing fingers and a new tree sprang up. Soon, where the bodies of the courageous slain lay, a copse of sixty Yews stood sentinel, a reminder of where the last battle had been fought and lost.

So the ancient Yews of Kingley Vale lived and lived and lived and lived, bound now to an unkind cycle of decay and rebirth and memory. Their branches grew down into the soil to form new stems. The trunks of the sixty trees rotted, but gave life within to new trees that grew and grew until they were indistinguishable from the root.

The years passed. The generations passed, the centuries passed in the endless pattern of silver springs and shimmering summers, golden autumns and hoary winters. But still men did not learn that death breeds only death. Little by little, the reputation of the Yew grew. Without wishing it, the Yew became a symbol of resurrection and hope, of wisdom. In Marden and Painswick, Clifton-upon-Teme and Iona, throughout the length and breadth of the country, the Yew became the favoured tree of the graveyard, of mourning, testament to the transience of memory and the frailty of human experience.

Twelve hundred years have passed since that first battle. Still, if you follow the path to the centre of Kingley Vale, the sixty stand untouched by sun or moon or rain. Their branches are gnarled, twisted like an old man's knuckles, their boughs are weary. Fingers, tendrils, trail the ground, touch the earth, paddle deep around in mossy roots and stippled bark. And within and above and around the wood, dwell green woodpeckers, red kites and buzzards, deer and stag, the chalkhill blue, holly blue and brimstone butterflies, so brief.

The people of Sussex fear to walk in the oldest part of the forest. They say that, at the winter solstice, the Yew trees whisper to one another, sing sibilant song of the folly of men. And so they do. Each year, when the shimmering spirits walk, if you listen carefully you will hear the trees speak of the hopes, the stories, the delusions of men, all the words they have captured in the seams of their leaves, the run of their branches, over the previous year. The indiscretions of human beings as they have come to the grove to walk, to pray, to weep, to climb, to rest, to wish.

These Yew trees are the oldest living things in the country. They wish it was not so. They would like to slide softly away, as can the ash and the oak and the elder. But human memory is brief, stupid, unconnected. Men have not yet learnt to live side by side, like the trees of the forest. So when the white winter dawn comes once more, and the solstice is over, the Yews sigh and stretch and settle back into their ancient selves once more.

For the length of an age.

Author's Note

This is one of four stories inspired by mythology or ancient legend. 'Why the Yew Tree Lives So Long' was commissioned in 2011 for a short story collection published in aid of the Woodland Trust. All proceeds raised went towards the charity which protects our woodlands.

Why Willows Weep was the brainchild of bestselling novelist Tracy Chevalier, who edited the collection which includes stories from Richard Mabey, Rachel Billington, Blake Morrison, Joanne Harris, Philippa Gregory, Tahmima Anam, Ali Smith and Philip Hensher. Each piece was inspired by a different tree – silver birch, oak, ash, beech – and with woodcut illustrations by Leanne Shapton.

I chose the yew trees of Kingley Vale, close to where I was born and grew up in Sussex. The oldest yew forest in Europe, there are many myths and legends associated with the nature reserve, not least that the oldest of the trees sprang up at the spot where the Saxon defenders of the Sussex Weald fell trying to hold back the Viking invasion of the ninth century.

SAINTE-THÉRÈSE

Montolieu, Languedoc, south-west France

Summer 2003

Sainte-Thérèse

Still, methinks,
There is an air comes from her: what fine chisel
Could ever yet cut breath?

Act V, Scene III, *The Winter's Tale*
WILLIAM SHAKESPEARE

In the blinking of an eye can the world shift. A pinprick of time that changes everything that has gone before it or will come after. Between one catch of breath and the next, the rest of forever defined by that single, solitary moment. For some it is a falling in love or a death or a song.

For Hermione, it was a saint.

*

They stopped in Montolieu for no better reason than Leon decided he'd had enough of the car. Even with all the windows wound down, like bitten nails, the heat had won. Parched brown fields stretched out in all directions as the road climbed higher up into the hills. Stumped plane trees, bark peeling and stained like liver spots, under which old men would play *boules* later in the day. The names of villages on signs – Alzonne, Pézens, Moussoulens – slashed through with a red line as you left the village. The occasional cluster of houses, but no sign of food or life. Nothing. Just the shimmering heat floating above the ribbon of tarmac.

As usual, Leon seemed to think it was her fault the morning hadn't gone well. For at least half an hour he had been picking away at her, criticising her map-reading skills, her organisational skills and . . . well her, in fact. It had taken her a while to accept he actually took pleasure in putting her down, making her seem stupid. Hermione knew that friends found his behaviour embarrassing and it made them feel awkward. She despised herself for putting up with it but, after ten years of marriage, their patterns were set. She no longer had the energy to argue back.

Habit, habit, thought Hermione, shifting in her seat. The leather sucked horribly under her legs. The irony was that her biggest fault, according to Leon, was that she was such a doormat. Always letting people take advantage of her. And now she had that familiar knotted feeling in her stomach, of tight nerves and disappointment at another day gone bad.

Hermione glanced at her watch, hearing the irritation in Leon's pointed silence. Twenty past eleven. She sighed, set her eyes on the middle distance and hoped for something to turn up, to make things go better.

*

The last bells of midday were clanging as they pulled into the village. Odd that a sound designed to gather people together should be so lonely, so plaintive. Montolieu looked like so many other of the pretty mountain places they'd passed through in this part of the Languedoc. Wooden shutters, opened just a crack to let in a little of the August heat. Elegant narrow stone houses that gave directly onto the street. Tubs of red geraniums on window ledges and on scrubbed stone steps. A heavy sense of stillness, a lack of hurry.

A romantic place, Hermione thought, the sort of place to discover hand in hand. She glanced at Leon, registering the beads of sweat on his upper lip and the patchwork of tiny red cuts from shaving, and sighed. Romantic with someone else, she corrected herself. Romantic in a book. She glanced at the guidebook open on her lap and saw that Montolieu was famous for its many bookshops. She opened her mouth to say something to break the silence, then stopped. Leon's expression made it obvious anything she said would be wrong.

She closed the book and looked out of the window.

A cock-eyed sign welcomed tourists to PARKING DE L'EGLISE. The capital letters made her want to shout the word aloud: L'EGLISE – THE CHURCH. Leon was frowning, concentrating so as not to bump the wheels of his precious Xantia on the high kerb. He pulled into the nearest space, killed the engine, then tapped his fingers three times on the steering wheel, like he always did: one, two, three. Was it pride at a task accomplished? An excess of nervous energy? Relief? Hermione had never been sure.

She was conscious of him jabbing at the switches to shut the roof and windows, aware of the soft whirring of mechanisms in motion, the clunk of each window arriving in place. All very subtle. All very top-of-the-range.

Until Leon got out of the car, still without saying a word, she hadn't thought he'd keep the sulk going. The sound of his door slamming was like a slap in the hot air. She assumed he was heading for the restaurant in the square opposite, but forced herself not to turn round in her seat to give him the satisfaction of seeing her watching.

Usually she'd feel upset, then blame herself for not averting it. But today, something inside her snapped. It was simply too hot and unfair and she couldn't summon the energy to move or follow or call out. She had done nothing wrong. She went along with what he wanted, did her best, but it was never good enough. Today, it didn't seem worth even trying.

She opened her door to let the air in, and sat quietly. Little by little, she started to feel better.

*

After fifteen minutes or so, she'd had her fill of the view and being looked at. Eyes behind net curtains. And if she stared any longer at the bizarre metal flamingos holding up the porch of the house opposite, Hermione knew she'd start laughing and would not be able to stop. In fact, she felt quite light-headed.

Finally, she glanced over to the square and saw Leon was sitting at a table, his back to the car, to her, drinking his wine and examining the menu with large look-at-me gestures. Hermione was surprised he hadn't gone ahead and ordered his meal too. He was waiting for her, she realised, having clearly decided to forgive and forget.

The normal pattern of things would be that Hermione would make the most of it. That she would hurry over and be grateful for the chance to put things right. But whether it was the sun or the stress of the holiday taking its toll, Hermione found herself rebelling. What, precisely, was she feeling grateful for? That he wasn't going to continue to be a pain? That he wasn't going to carry on behaving unreasonably?

She wouldn't do it. Not today. Today Leon could wait. Wonder where she'd got to. Perhaps even worry something might have happened to her? The thought of it made her feel powerful. She was standing up for herself. He could wait.

Hermione got out of the car and turned to the church itself. It was the only place that looked open. She'd have a quick look inside. She was not a manipulative woman, but the idea came to her – if Leon complained at how long she'd kept him waiting for lunch – that she'd say she assumed he'd be pleased she was taking an interest in the local architecture.

The thought made her smile.

It was an ugly building. Fourteenth century? Fifteenth, maybe? Gargoyles with lewd mouths squatted around the edges of the roof. Unpleasant. Years of having her appearance criticised had made her self-conscious, so Hermione found herself pressing her T-shirt to her chest as if the stone watchers were leering down her cleavage. She pulled at her shorts too, to reveal less orange-peeled thigh. Leon said the backs of her legs were ugly.

Hermione didn't want to go in, not really. She didn't much like churches. But the thought of Leon watching her dither compelled her to hitch up her bag on to her shoulder and walk with purpose to the wooden door. It had a clumsy iron latch, the sort you'd expect to find in a National Trust cottage. She pushed down with her thumb. It didn't move. She tried again, this time giving the door a vicious little kick with her foot. A creak and she was in.

*

The ecclesiastical chill slipped over Hermione's bare arms and legs, the lingering smell of a Sunday service and damp.

As her eyes got used to the gloom, she realised that the church was much bigger than it appeared from the outside. Metal chandeliers hung from the rafters like fake wagon wheels in a country pub. Scenes of the crucifixion covered the walls, the reds and blues obscene against the grey of the stone. Beneath each tableau, thin candles burned in rows, their yellow flames giving no light or warmth. Faded scraps of paper were pinned on the walls, curt instructions on what to do and how to behave. Light a candle, drop a *centime* in the box. Pray for me.

Remember me.

Hermione supposed that her discomfort would fade once she was inside, playing the bona fide tourist, but in fact she felt nervous. One of 'her headaches', as Leon would put it. She put it down to the heat and too little to drink.

Clasping her hands in front of her, Hermione began to walk around with that shuffle particular to churches and art galleries, slow and steady and serious. The slap of her leather sandals was embarrassingly loud on the flagstones and the only sound except for the tick, tick of the electricity meter above the door.

Nerves sloshed at the pit of her stomach, intensifying with every step she took. Everything seemed unpleasant, threatening, rather than interesting. All these scenes of suffering and torture, nothing of faith or forgiveness. The pulpit seemed to lurch out from one of the pillars in the nave like a twisted dragon and when she screwed up her eyes, to test the truth of what she was seeing, she saw only images of hell and retribution.

The side chapel was no more pleasant, like a room in a giant doll's house, three-sided with the front open to the nave.

Wallpaper, broken furniture and everyday relics peppering the altars – an empty vase, flat-topped glass cases protecting scraps of material and feathers.

Protecting them from whom? From what? Those who came to worship unseen? It all repulsed her, made her want to smash it to pieces. She realised that she was twisting her wedding ring on her finger, round and round, making the skin underneath the gold sore and red.

By now, it was only the thought of Leon and the scene to come that was keeping Hermione in the church. She couldn't shake the idea she was being watched, the sense of activity just suspended, as if she'd interrupted something. She imagined that, as soon as she left, the air would whoosh back into place behind her. More than once she spun round, sure that someone else was there – a tourist who'd slipped in without her hearing or a local woman come to polish or pray – but there was no one.

Hermione found herself standing at the communion rail. She lifted her head and saw a bleeding Christ, nailed to his cross, and a starched white altar cloth embroidered with greens and golds. More oppressive was the army of plaster statues, like a fossilised congregation, stationed between her and the altar.

Their paint was ragged round the edges, chipped pastel pinks and yellows and sea-green. Saint André, Sainte Germana, Saint Jean, Saint Antoine, adult faces on three-quarter size bodies, as if they'd stopped growing before time. One in a monk's robe, a naked baby in one hand and a Bible in the other. One leaning on a staff, a lamb warming his dead feet. One clutching a skeleton's hand, sharp like a claw. But most of all it was their dead eyes, their claustrophobic eyes, which pressed into her, accusing her, judging her.

Suddenly, Hermione couldn't bear it a moment longer. Overwhelmed by a need to get out of the church, she turned and ran back down the nave, her leather sandals slipping on the smooth stones. Where was the door, why couldn't she find the door? And still the eyes were burning into her back, challenging her to stand her ground, to stand up for herself. But she'd forgotten how.

She didn't see Sainte Thérèse until it was too late. Hermione collided with the statue. Dazed, she touched her forehead with shocked fingers and found she was bleeding. She couldn't make sense of it. How could she possibly have missed seeing the statue when she came in? It was so much bigger than the others and set right in front of the door.

She raised her head.

The plaster face of the saint wore an expression of such serenity, such grace, that Hermione's fear evaporated. She felt her shoulders drop and heard a sigh, of relief or contentment, slip from between her lips. A cobweb was caught between the fingers on Sainte Thérèse's right hand which cradled the outline of a quill. No longer frightened, Hermione found herself reaching up to brush it away. It was an act of such intimacy, she found herself blushing.

And in that moment, no more than a pinprick of time, she was touched by a presence that was white and clear, as if something pure had crept inside her head and was pushing out all other sensations. Such lightness, such stillness. An absence of physical being, a calm and peaceful silence that seemed to go on for ever.

For a moment, she was looking into living eyes. Thérèse looking at her. Hermione smiled.

Then, it was over. Just the grey of the church and the tick,

tick of the electricity meter and herself, alone again, but at peace. Hermione had no idea what had happened, only that something had. And even though she didn't believe in living saints or spirits, she knew that her world had shifted.

Hermione pushed the hair out of her eyes, picked up her handbag, then opened the door and walked out into the Midi sun. Lost in the shadows or an act of deliberation, she did not notice her wedding ring lying on the cold floor at the feet of the saint.

*

Years later, friends would still talk about how Hermione came back from that French holiday a different woman. About how strange it was that, after years of putting up with Leon's bullying and belittling, she'd had the courage to send him packing. Walked out of a church in a place called Montolieu, called a taxi to the airport in Toulouse, bought a new ticket and flown home on her own. It was as if she'd got a new lease of life, they said. As if she'd got a bit of her old spirit back, they said.

You could see it in her eyes.

Author's Note

Along with 'Red Letter Day', this is another of the earliest stories I wrote set in the Languedoc.

In the 1990s, when we were discovering Carcassonne, we spent many summer weekends driving from village to village, exploring the region. We fell in love with Montolieu – known as the 'village of books' – a pretty place north-west of Carcassonne. Like most French towns in the Aude, large and small, the church is at the heart of the community and unlike their Protestant counterparts, Catholic churches are usually colourful affairs – plaster saints, vivid paintings, richly decorated.

There are several Saint Teresas. Saint Teresa d'Ávila, a sixteenth-century Spanish saint, has a quill and book as her symbol and, among her various responsibilities, she is the patron saint of those in need of grace.

Reading this again after ten years – and after the publication of *Labyrinth*, *Sepulchre* and *Citadel* – I found it interesting to see how I was already trying out themes that were to become so important to me: the connection of history and emotion; the idea that architecture and landscape influences storytelling; the sense that reality can be momentarily suspended.

A version of this story was first published in *Woman & Home* magazine in 2005.

THE SHIP OF THE DEAD

Finistère, Brittany Coast
November 1930

The Ship of the Dead

Sur le Raz de Sein, au crépuscule, apparaît parfois un bateau qui navigue sans sillage toutes voiles dehors contre vents et marées.

Sometimes at dusk, between the mainland and the island of Sein, a boat appears that leaves no wake, its sails all unfurled, indifferent to wind or tide.

BRETON LEGEND

Although the night was dark – no moon and the sky obscured by cloud – I was able to follow the pale pathway worn by generations of feet in the cliff top. The crash of the waves on rocks and the suck of the tide on shingle far below kept me on course.

The land rose and I followed the track, the flint and chalk faint but unmistakable in the turf. I had walked further than I had intended and I was weary, but at last I reached the summit of the headland and looked out over what I knew to be the ocean. Nothing between me and the Americas.

I sat on a well situated boulder and contemplated my solitude, regretting I was walking alone. I was not – have never been – a clubbable sort. All the same, I enjoyed the pleasure of the right sort of companion. On this occasion, not one of my acquaintances had been available to undertake a walking tour of the Finistère coastline – for me, a return to the happy landscape of my childhood – so I had been obliged to travel alone.

I took out my tobacco pouch alone and smoked a pipe. It is said that tobacco deters insects and that may be true in some climates and latitudes. But here, on the Atlantic coast of Brittany, it had the opposite effect. I was soon beset by a cloud of hovering midges, many of them bloodthirsty, all of them irritating and oppressive. It quite spoiled my mood of contemplation.

I knocked out my pipe on the stone, stood up, adjusted my rucksack onto my shoulders, set my grip firm around my stick of hazel, and moved on.

The descent was no easier than the climb. The path was slippery beneath my boots – not from moisture, but from the small stones and gravel that I sent skittering down the steep slope ahead of me with every tread.

Just then, a pale moon was revealed by a rent in the clouds and I saw I was now walking along the edge of a field, lined with a drystone wall separating me from a substantial drop to a distant beach frilled with foam from the breaking waves. Wondering how deep might be the drop, I picked a stone and threw it as far as I could out into the night. I was able to count full to twelve before I heard a faint click. I have never suffered from a fear of heights nor am I usually prone to flights of fancy, but it seemed to me that a breeze sprang up all at once, a plaintive sound, deliberate and demanding, like a vexed child, provoking in my imagination the idea that I had transgressed by hurling the pebble. That its proper place was among its fellows in the wall, no doubt erected to prevent grazing animals from falling to their deaths. The idea caused me to shiver. All at once, I was keen to be off the cliff-top path and installed in some boarding house or shelter for the night.

At the bottom of the dip was a fingerpost indicating routes in three different directions: one indicating the way I had come, the second a pathway that led inland, and the third, a continuation of the cliff-top path. I suppose that had I taken the route away from the sea, I would have found shelter of some kind, if only a bothy for sheep or goats, but I was inclined to follow the wall and see where it would take me.

The land was rising again, though less steeply, and at the next crest I was gratified to see lights in the distance. The wind grew stronger still as I trudged down the long descent towards the village. The ragged curtain of cloud drew back revealing the stars, allowing my tired eyes to perceive more of the landscape. Something about the play of darkness and sea tides and moon-shine imbued everything with a dusty, earthy pallor. Rather than a rich blue in the firmament and grey and charcoal and black of shadows on the land, this part of the world seemed to be clothed in the rough habit of a Franciscan monk.

I focused on the lights of the village and quickened my step. Soon enough I realised I had made a mistake taking this path. It was the hardest walking I had yet undertaken. The village was down on the beach, by my reckoning some one hundred feet below the cliff path. There was a precarious stairway, cut roughly into the escarpment, the steps lined with a mixture of timber and, here and there, flat stones. Even so, I wondered whether the risk was worth the potential reward – a warm bed under cover. But the memory of the strange wailing of the wind persuaded me. I did not want to pass the night on the exposed path on the cliffs.

I began to descend, one awkward step at a time, my hands grasping at tussocks of wiry, salt-loving grass. Halfway down I rested for a moment on a kind of ledge. The tide was out and the beach an enormous pale crescent of perfect smooth sand, glistening in the starlight. Below, at the foot of the stair, were the unmistakable hulks of fishing boats drawn up on to higher ground to keep them out of the water and it entered my mind that, should there be no welcome for me in the village, I might shelter well enough beneath one of these until morning.

Finally, I reached the easier terrain. Rough grass bordered the sand. Away to the left, on the south side of the bay, I counted thirteen lights in the cluster of indistinct shapes that were all I could make out of the low houses.

I walked a curved path around the edge of the beach and was within twenty yards or so of the first of the buildings when a vague movement of shadow upon darkness caused me to stop. I cannot say why my hand went to my chest or why I held my breath – why shouldn't someone be there at the fringe of the sand? He had, no doubt, more right than I to be there.

Gathering my wits, I realised it was only the form of a man, kneeling low to the ground, tending to a sheep. The animal was lying badly and I surmised it must have fallen from the cliff. They do say that sheep, of all creatures, seek death. Disturbed by my presence, the man lifted his head. I saw that he was gaunt and that his eyes were black. I was about to speak – I know a few words of the local dialect – when the animal let out a pitiful screech.

My few words of Breton deserted me and, stupidly, I heard myself speaking to the man instead in French. Asking if I could be of assistance. He paid me no more attention than the rocks pay to the tide.

Paralysed in some kind of embarrassment and horror, I watched him remove his coat and wrap it around the animal's muzzle and lean the full weight of his body on its flank. I glanced up, abruptly aware of the oddity of the scene. There was no one else about, but when I looked to the village, I saw a rectangle of light open up in one of the dark low houses and the silhouette of a man appear in the doorway. He called out, something I could not hear, and my man called out in reply.

I recognised the word for 'dead'.

The door slammed shut and I don't know why, but it seemed the action of shutting out the night was hurried, as if to place a barrier between the inhabitants of the house and some danger.

The sheep twitched for a final time. The man murmured re-assuring words that I could not distinguish or understand, all the time gently patting and stroking at the animal's thin shoulder and flank.

Escorting the animal to its death.

Feeling it would be, somehow, bad manners to leave, I waited. The wind that had felt so brisk at the top of the cliffs now seemed little more than a whisper.

Finally, both the man and the creature were still. I introduced myself once again and, this time, he acknowledged me with a few words in the local dialect, one of which I recognised as the Breton for 'stranger'. I gave him my well-rehearsed paragraph of introduction – that I was walking the coast for the purposes of preparing to write a memoir in honour of my late grandfather who had grown up in the region and whose first language was now spoken by a diminishing brotherhood of isolated fishing villages.

He listened politely, though without sign of particular interest. I pressed on.

'So I would be grateful for somewhere to stay the night, a bed or a chair – even a dry floor.'

He nodded slowly, unwrapped his leather coat from around the muzzle of the sheep and put it back on, pushing his arms into its heavy sleeves. With strong hands he took hold of the animal's hooves and lifted it from the ground, hooking it up onto his shoulders. Then, without speaking, he turned and set off towards the village. His behaviour seemed to indicate I should follow him.

We passed between the houses in silence, the gaunt man treading steadily ahead of me. Here and there our feet crunched on shingle, but we were otherwise silent upon the sand and hardy grass. All the doors were closed, although one or two windows remained open. Smoke rose from several of the chimneys, despite the relative warmth of the evening.

In the centre of the village was a small open space with what looked like a shrine. An orange glow from an unshuttered window cast an ugly gleam across a stone effigy of some saint, no doubt reputed to bring good fortune to all those who trade and fish upon the sea.

Then, a door was flung open and two children ran out into the darkness, laughing and calling one another names. The boy held something in his hand and stretched on tiptoe, keeping it well out of reach of his sister. A woman appeared in the doorway, a mother or grandmother. Her expression was impossible to see against the light of the oil lamp inside the house, but I recognised the distinctive starched bonnet of the region, spotless in stiff white linen standing out in broad wings either side of her head.

'Good evening,' I said.

There was an abrupt change in atmosphere. The woman

barked a command and the children left off their game and scuttled back indoors without a moment's hesitation. She remained where she was and did not acknowledge my companion.

He moved forward, bowed low by the dead weight of the dead animal across his shoulders. I made to follow, but he shook his head. Assuming him to be having second thoughts at having offered me shelter for the night, I made to reassure him I only intended to stay a single night, when the woman interrupted.

'Not with him. You may stay with us.'

'But . . .'

I turned to my companion, but he was already walking on.

I watched him leave, realising that the decision had been made for me.

'Well, in which case, thank you. I am grateful.' I began my explanation. 'I am walking the cliff top path in memory—'

She cut across me again. 'Come indoors, stranger.'

I smiled and told her my name. Her expression was neutral, neither welcoming nor resentful, yet I hesitated to enter. My gaze followed the gaunt man. He was some way further forward now, moving towards the last dwelling among the low houses at the edge of the village. In the silence of the evening, I heard the sliding of a wooden bolt. The door opened and he disappeared inside.

'Come indoors,' she said again.

It was an uncomfortable evening. The household was evidently poor and I felt obliged to share the food I had set aside for evening meal. There was a salty green vegetable, much like samphire, to stretch the meagre fare, but no bread. It would have been enough for my own needs, but not sustaining when stretched to feed two hungry children, a grown woman and a tired man.

Growing up on the Left Bank in Paris, I had visited my country grandfather on many occasions. Although I had never learnt the language to any degree of fluency, it seemed to me then that I had an affinity with the people of these distant cliffs, headlands and bays. However, in this modest house, I struggled to find common ground and we exchanged little conversation. She found it hard to understand the dialect that I employed, or perhaps my accent was too difficult for her. Either way, I was grateful when she indicated I should sleep in a hammock strung between two sturdy posts.

Perhaps it was the hunger in my stomach or, possibly, I was overtired, but I tossed and turned as the hours passed. The two small windows had no shutters and my sleepy eye perceived the lightening of the sky. Somewhere around dawn I heard a boat putting out upon the water, close at hand. I remember thinking to myself that the tide must be in.

Finally, I slept.

*

I woke to an empty house.

I dressed and went outside, rubbing tooth powder on my teeth with my forefinger. I suppose I must have given the impression of foaming at the mouth for the two young children left off mending nets and pointed and laughed. I roared and pretended to be an ogre, which they found the most remarkable and entertaining sight.

I sat with them for a little while, impressed with the nimbleness of their tiny fingers. Had I met the two children in the fifth *arrondissement* I would have estimated their ages at seven and five. They may have been older. Here, in the harsh environment of the World's End of Finistère, children grow up small. Some never attain even average height for a well-nourished city dweller.

I was hungry so, after a while, I left the children and prowled about the village, seeking some occupation that might cause me to be invited to share in their meals.

There was an onshore wind. Out at sea, a reef of black rocks seemed to bar the entrance to the bay. All the same, standing on the dense wet sand, I could see four fishing boats out on the sparkling water, sailing a channel between the reef and the grey smudge of an island still further out, perfectly situated to protect the settlement from the worst of the weather in times of storm. There was a wild beauty to it, a romance, I suppose, and I made a rash promise to myself that, should I stay in the village for any length of time, I should try and obtain passage to the island.

I had not been watching for long when, one after another, I observed the fishing boats start for home, confidently picking a path between the dangerous rocks. I took off my boots and socks, rolled up my trousers and left my jacket on a tussock and joined the others at the water's edge waiting to help bringing the vessels up onto the sand.

As is usually the case with honest physical labour, my assistance was welcome. In these places where the end of each day of toil is greeted with a sigh of relief and a respite for stiff and weary muscles, a burden shared is not intemperately refused.

Between us, we brought three boats safely in. Their owners were soon engaged in sorting the catch. A fire had been laid on the beach and three women were heating a quantity of broth in a vast iron cauldron, blackened by years of use, which hung from a weary frame. Chilled by the onshore breeze, I stepped closer to the flames and watched the last boat dodging through the reef.

For reasons I did not immediately perceive, the atmosphere changed. The watchers on the beach were aware that something was awry. Had I been asked, I suppose I would have noted that the fourth boat was taking a slightly different route from the previous three, but there seemed to be no danger. Nevertheless, one of the women ran down to the surf and called out in a high shrill voice, almost a song, waving her arms above her head that the captain should steer to port.

The men, too, were now calling out to one another and raced across the beach, heading for a sandbank that stretched out like a finger into the waves. I followed them. Sure enough the fourth boat, carried onshore with too much way by the wind, ran aground. The hull creaked and groaned as it climbed the sandbank. There was a danger of terminal damage and a catastrophic loss of livelihood for the fisherman and his family.

The men plunged into the water knee and thigh deep and braced themselves to push the boat off with the next wave. I joined them, though missing my footing and found myself immersed to my waist. We braced ourselves to take the weight of the boat and the power of the water and wind behind it.

It was almost too much for our several strengths. Luckily the craft had only a shallow draught. We held it and, as the water receded, managed to combine in a great shove so that the wave carried the boat bobbing away to safety. I was congratulated for my efforts and returned to the beach as a valued member of the crew.

While we had been occupied in the water, the women had

been turning the pot. I stood by the fire to dry my sodden clothes and saw a thick rich stew of root vegetables, green leaves and fish of several species, gutted but otherwise whole.

We ate standing up. Had we been in Paris, at a table dressed with good linen, they would have found me a squeamish companion. On this occasion I had no such qualms. I picked and sucked at the bones, relishing every mouthful and following the lead of the other villagers in tossing the skeletons and other indigestible parts into the flames.

Satisfied at last, I looked about for a drink. The stew was salty and I felt the need of a cup of cool water to slake my thirst. It was then that I saw him, the gaunt man that I had met at the foot of the steps.

All morning I hadn't given him a thought, despite the fact he had been first to welcome me to the village, and I felt awkward for it.

At first I imagined he had come to share the communal meal, but I was wrong. He walked across the beach, passing within ten paces of the small community of us clustered about the great iron cauldron.

No one acknowledged him. Not one turned their head nor followed him with their eyes. I wondered if I was the only man who could see him or, rather, that only I was prepared to admit his presence. Indeed, all the time he remained in earshot, the gentle thrum of conversation became subdued. Only when he had disappeared, clambering among the rocks and pools at the northern edge of the bay, did the atmosphere become convivial once more. I wanted to ask who he was, why he was shunned, but not wanting to disturb the new-found friendship between us all, I remained silent.

Taking my leave a little later, I picked up my belongings

and returned to the little house. No one was there, but I was pleased to find two earthenware jugs of drinking water standing ready on a rudimentary sideboard, each with a square of muslin draped across the top. I took the tin cup from my rucksack and consumed a pint and a half of fresh clear water.

I stood still for a moment and was visited by an intense feeling of satisfaction. I felt quite at ease in this community. The landscape reminded me of the pleasant summer days of childhood. The limitations of our shared language suited both my temperament and my mood.

My clothes were dry in part, from standing in front of the fire, so I draped them on the chair back and climbed into the hammock. In my hands were my notebook and my favourite all-weather pencil – a very hard lead that lasted a long time without sharpening. It was my firm intention to write up the experiences I'd had in the village and make good my promise to my dear grandfather. Later, I looked back at the page and discovered I had only written seven words before falling asleep. Those words were in themselves unimportant, though they serve as a reminder that, at that stage, I was unaware of the name of the village in which I found myself.

*

It has never been my habit to sleep in the daytime. On this occasion, however, night had fallen by the time I woke.

The family were still absent, though they had clearly returned during the afternoon. A lamp was now burning and my clothes had been spread more carefully on the sparse furniture.

I dressed and went out into the dusk. There was no one to be seen. All the low houses were dark. The only window that showed a light was the distant cabin that stood apart from the other dwellings, home to the gaunt man.

In the absence of any other company, I walked up the hill and knocked on his door. There was a brief sound of shuffling, then the door opened. He stared, then stood aside without a word and closed the door quietly behind me.

It is hard to do justice to what I saw. The place was a hovel, certainly, though it did not feel unwelcoming. There was just one room. The floor was beaten earth. The timber walls were all lined with wool, whole fleeces stitched together with what looked like lengths of gut. From the ceiling hung a myriad fragments of what I first took to be carved wood, dangling on slender threads.

He gestured to me to sit down. There was only one seat, a bench formed by the broad trunk of some tree. He stood opposite me, his head on one side. He seemed reluctant to speak, though I felt he was glad of my company.

Then at last he cleared his throat.

'I was a sailor,' he said.

He made this statement three times, at first in a curious dialect, then in a Breton that I could understand. Finally he repeated himself in what seemed to me to be a southern European language – perhaps Catalan or even Levantine. I had lived for a short time in Alexandria and it seemed reminiscent of the argot of the sailors I encountered there.

'You have travelled widely?' I asked.

I realised that I had fallen into French. To my surprise, he continued in the same tongue.

'I have travelled widely, from this bay to the island and back again.'

'I prefer to feel the hard earth beneath my boots.'

He was silent for a while. I waited.

'I was eighteen years old when the call came. Since that time I have been shunned.'

I was uncertain what he meant by this, though I had guessed as much. I wondered if he had committed some dreadful crime in his youth. It wouldn't be uncommon in these parts for his fellows to make him suffer for it long after the memory of his transgression had ceased to mean anything to the living. These close-knit communities can be harsh and unforgiving judges.

I waited for him to say more, but he showed no sign of speaking further. I began to wonder how old he might be. His severely lined face and sunken cheeks gave an impression of a man in his sixties at least, but those who live by the sea age quickly, then live on an unconscionable time.

He took up a tidy knife and began paring at a pale object, carving an intricate design into its length. In the poor light of the single lamp, I couldn't make out the shapes that his knife revealed, but I recognised the pale object as bone, probably the shin of a sheep – perhaps the very same animal that had fallen from the cliff path the previous evening.

He saw me paying close attention to his work and waved a hand towards the ceiling. I stood up and peered at the nearest carvings. I saw they were all bone. There is a peculiar quality to the material that makes it different from any wood that I have ever encountered or seen worked.

He handed me the lamp. I inspected the hanging ornaments more closely and gasped. Tiny faces, no larger than my littlest fingernail, perhaps smaller still, carved with extraordinary precision. The minuscule faces were disconcertingly lifelike. My eye was drawn from one to another, dozens of them, all different, all finely worked.

How many were there? I am certain at least a hundred bones dangled from the struts supporting the roof. Each seemed to accommodate at least six or seven likenesses. Each likeness projected a distinct personality. And as I passed the lamp from hand to hand, they seemed to come to life. The play of the light across them transformed their expressions, from despair to fury, from resignation to horror.

I felt faint and feared I might fall. I put out a hand to steady myself, but the only fixed object in the room I could use to maintain my balance was the gaunt man himself and he shrank from my touch.

On that instant, the door burst open and the room was suddenly crowded with men. Strong arms grabbed me and lifted me from my feet, carrying me out into the night without explanation. I protested, but they paid no heed and did not stop until we arrived at the cauldron on the beach.

A few embers were still glowing and they deposited me alongside the fire. I was still light-headed, but the cool sand and the fresh air revived me and I found my tongue.

'What is the meaning of this? I am not used to being manhandled.'

No one paid the slightest attention. I tried to get to my feet but my head swam and the vision of all the horrible little faces seemed to surround me like a white swarm of slow-moving horseflies.

I sat back and rubbed my hands over my eyes, feeling sick to my boots.

'How did you know I was there?'

Still, no one spoke to me or offered explanation. Frustrated, I resolved at least to take out my notebook and make a complete record of this strange settlement.

By now, all but one of the men who had seized me from the cabin had drifted away. He looked a solid citizen, with broad shoulders and a handsome square face. I recognised him from the adventure with the fishing boat that ran aground. He knelt beside me and looked into my eyes.

'Will you tell me?' I said, attempting the Breton language.

The man replied in rudimentary, strongly accented French. 'Do not speak to him. Not speak.'

I felt a spurt of anger on the gaunt man's behalf, even though I did not know his story.

'You have made him an outcast, yes I see that. But why? What crime has he committed to be punished in this way?'

He was frowning, whether because he didn't understand the words or because he didn't understand why I should be asking the question, I cannot be sure.

'Do not speak,' he insisted.

His intransigence made me more belligerent still.

'I'm not from this village. I shall speak to whomsoever I please.'

He shook his head. 'No,' he shouted. 'No.'

'Why should I not speak to him? It's cruel, I tell you.'

'That man he is . . .' He spread his hands wide to indicate he had no words.

I shrugged, though I admit my interest was piqued. 'Say it in your language. Perhaps I will understand.'

He took a deep breath. 'He is Ankou.'

My blood went cold and though I had heard quite clearly, I made him repeat it.

'I beg your pardon?'

'Ankou,' he said again. 'You understand?'

I had learnt of the Ankou at my grandfather's knee. It was

a ludicrous folk tale with no foundation in fact; even so, there was something in the man's demeanour that gave me pause for thought.

'Yes,' I told him. 'I understand.'

'He transports the dead.'

*

My grandfather told me that a legend is a story about someone who may have existed far back in some distant past, whilst a myth is a story that is, by general agreement, a fiction, with no connection to real people, however far back one might search.

He had told me many such stories. Living at the tip of the great Brittany peninsular, summer visits had introduced me to all kinds of fantastic creatures – imps, giants, naiads and sages – each associated with a detail of the coastline or the sea. And the Ankou: a fisherman called by name in the deep of the night by God or the Devil to transport dead souls to the portal of the beyond on the shore of the distant island.

That evening, sitting alone on the hard sand, I thought of how my grandfather had shaped my sensibilities. It was thanks to him that I enjoyed gardening, mostly the growing of food but also, from time to time, flowers and shrubs. He taught me to cook with the produce of his own soil, to set traps for vermin such as rabbits and to carry out repairs about the home. In short, it was his influence that transformed me from a boy into a capable young man.

Because I had slept the entire afternoon I was not in the least tired. The moon was low, almost touching the horizon of the sea, and appeared enormous. Otherwise the sky was veiled with cloud and the air was relatively warm. The cooking utensils had been cleaned and were stacked on a clean board alongside the cooking fire. The heavy iron cauldron retained some of its warmth.

The fishermen would go out once more upon an early tide, so I had no expectation of finding any society in the village. All the same, I rose to my feet and strolled between the squat houses. Here and there I noticed a job to be done – for example guttering that was poorly attached, allowing the rain to run down the wall. I was plunged into a reverie in which I made myself indispensable to this small community of isolated peasants and became a fixture in their lives.

I came to a halt in the centre of the modest cluster of houses, alongside the rustic shrine. In the silvery light I saw that the saint – if saint it was – took the figure of a mariner. I supposed this was unsurprising: what would one expect in a fishing village? But there were some peculiarities that emerged on closer study.

The skill of the stonemason had depicted a thin man standing upright in the aft of a fishing boat, his eye fixed upon the horizon. I turned in order to follow his gaze and realised that it was focused upon the distant island beyond the reef of black rocks. That said, one might just as well have argued that his gaze was fixed upon the moon. The line to each was more or less the same.

At the base of the carving, the artist had rendered an image of the mariner's boat. It was depicted on the angle and it seemed that an attempt had been made to give a sense of the movement of the craft over the waves.

I was unsure what time it was and was resolved to return to the woman and her children once more, when I heard a sound I recognised from the previous evening. The sliding of the wooden bolt that fastened the door of the cabin at the far end of the village.

I stood in silence and soon heard the steady tread of the gaunt man coming towards me. He was dressed as he had been at that first meeting. He carried nothing in his hands and paid no attention to me as he passed, although I must have been visible to him, standing in the open by the light of a strong moon.

Was it to prove I was a man of the city? That I paid no heed to old wives' tales? Or that I wished to demonstrate I would not be dictated to about to whom I should or should not talk? I cannot say, only that all at once the idea returned to me of visiting the island. If my original companion was preparing to take a boat out onto the water, could I not persuade him to take me with him? Morning was nearly upon us and I could enjoy the sunrise on sparkling water between the reef and the landmass out on the open sea.

'I say,' I called.

He did not slacken his pace. I hurried after him. 'I say, will you take me out with you?'

Still, he did not even turn his head.

'I know enough about the water. I won't be a burden to you.'

At that he turned his mournful gaze upon me. It was impossible to read his eyes, so deep-set were they above his prominent cheekbones.

I hurried on. 'Since I have been here, I find I have formed an attachment to the place. I would be very grateful to visit the island out there in the ocean.'

We were already part-way down the beach and as we stood, one facing the other, I wondering if I had made myself understood. Then, with the smallest movement of his right hand, he indicated a boat that already sat bobbing in the water. I took his gesture for acquiescence.

'Thank you. You are very kind.'

Together we crossed the sand to the fringe of surf. I hesitated, intending to take off my boots and roll up my trousers but he pressed on into the water, so I did the same.

I took hold of the prow to keep the boat steady as he climbed aboard and then swung my own leg over the gunwales. It was a fine solid craft, perhaps nine metres in length, with a single mast rigged and ready for the wind. He stood in the aft and took hold of the tiller and I realised that, by some action of the tide, we were already drifting away from the shore.

Then I felt the boat rock as if something or someone had come on board, though the gaunt man himself had not moved. His head was turned, looking out towards the reef. All at once, I suddenly had a sense of misgiving. Not because I gave credence to the superstitions of the village, but rather wondering if it was wise to be out upon the water in darkness.

But it was too late now. The boat gave another lurch and swung round. We were under way. The prow came in line with the route that I had seen the fishing boats take through the reef, though the boat still rolled from side to side as if a multitude of travellers were hauling themselves over the beam.

I had the sense of no longer being alone. A disquieting claustrophobia began to take hold of me and I shrank in on myself. I felt my muscles contract as I tucked in my elbows against my flanks. And with each sway of the boat, it sat deeper in the water. Perhaps we were holed and would soon sink. I dipped my hand into the bilge, expecting it to be at least a foot deep in seawater. All I found was a short length of damp rope.

The sail billowed, taking the wind. We began to pick up

speed. It struck me that this was the first offshore breeze that I had encountered on this coastline. There was no need to tack or even, or so it seemed, to steer. The boat made rapid way and the gaunt man's hand rested only lightly upon the tiller.

Sitting in the prow, I felt the slap of the water against the hull and spray on my face. As we met each wave, I expected the black water to cascade over the sides and swill about around my booted feet, but it didn't.

I looked over the edge, down into the dark waves. Here and there in the water I thought that I saw shapes, like the figures of men, pale and indistinct in the moonlight, their hands reaching up and out, but before they could take hold of the timbers and haul themselves aboard, we had moved on. Then I heard the strange and plaintive wailing that, on the cliff top, had accompanied my arrival into the village the previous night.

It was as if a veil had been lifted from my eyes. I was caught between horror and wonder for our boat was now crowded with those taken by the sea. The drowned. They stood shoulder to shoulder, massed like rotting corn left too long in the fields. I was transfixed by their awful faces, sagging and collapsing in every stage of decomposition and decay, rags for clothes, limbs torn and broken, fleshless fingers flailing at the night. The swell became deeper and they jostled against one another. I began to hear their voices, despairing and complaining, but with a note of restrained joy whose reason I could not fathom.

I wondered what kind of madness had enraptured me. Was I asleep in the hammock? Had I eaten the flesh of some hallucinogenic fish? I had no idea if such a thing existed. Or perhaps it was the herbs, the green leaves with which the stew was flavoured?

No, it couldn't be. I could feel the spray on my cheeks and taste the salt on my lips. Whatever was happening had to be true. Simultaneously, I knew it could not be real.

We were nearly at the reef. Another silvery hand tried to reach up and take hold of the craft as it passed. An angry murmur went up from the ghastly passengers. One of the long-dead reached out a claw-like hand and beat the other away. It fell back into the water with a terrible moaning sound of renunciation and loss.

'Why can the others not come aboard?' I shouted.

The question was absurd. They were mirages, surely, a play of the moonlight upon the water. But I persisted.

'If some can be transported to the afterlife, why not all?'

I saw his lips move but could not hear his voice.

'Please, tell me,' I cried.

His lips moved again and, this time, the tightly packed drowned turned towards him. In parody of some ghastly stage routine, they began to whisper together and turn. First those closest to him repeated his low words, then they passed the message to a neighbour who turned and passed it on again. In that way, the message travelled down the boat from gaping mouth to mangled ear, until all the appalling faces, blue and white and bloated, were hissing it at me in ragged unison, each it seemed in a separate language, but all of them comprehensible to me by some demonic alchemy.

'They have not yet earned their deliverance. Might not ever do so . . .'

I fell back in the prow of the boat. It was true. He was the Ankou and I had embarked upon the Ship of the Dead.

There was a moment of silence followed by a faint cry of hollow triumph. We were through the reef and out in the open sea. The wind drove us on. We sat so low in the water that it rose in a wall of darkness to either side.

The dead souls became excited. They grimaced and turned to one another, mouthing incomprehensible words. Our pace slowed, the great wake subsided and the island became visible, at first just a black shadow on the night, then more and more distinct. I soon made out trees and a beach.

There we headed.

The drowned edged forward. Those closest to me wanted my place in the prow. They leaned in, almost touching my garments. Those further back shuffled forward too, pressing up against their fellows, until soon I was completely hemmed in by the foul and rotting bodies. They groped with their terrible hands past my face, scratching their bony claws through the night air, as if the gesture would make the island come more rapidly near.

Through the thicket of decomposing flesh, I saw the gaunt villager stand and raise his hand. There was the unmistakable grinding of hull on shore. We had arrived.

Immediately, they began to leave. Clambering over me in their haste to quit the boat and reach the land, I was trampled and buffeted by their vile remains. Ten then twenty then thirty and more, kicking and dragging themselves over the prow and splashing away through the shallows to the beach.

Speechless with horror, I covered my head with my hands and curled myself into a ball for fear of contamination or injury. The truth is, I felt no pain – their touch was insubstantial – but it left a nausea, a deep, disconcerting revulsion. I cursed myself for having come. In my need to prove myself better than the villagers and their ancient superstitions, I had brought this dreadful experience upon myself.

They staggered from the water, took a few steps upon the land before coming to a halt and raising their hands. I heard their joyful voices like the yelps of distant dogs, as they began to fade. I cannot say precisely when their substance disintegrated utterly into darkness.

Without the gaunt man even seeming to turn the boat around, we were all at once again riding the white crests. We got into trouble in a spiralling eddy from which our boat was flung. The prow swung violently round and, without any kind of wind, as if moved by some mysterious underwater force, the boat began to drive homeward towards the shore. The gaunt villager lay back against the timbers and the tiller swung wildly back and forth. Unburdened of our cargo, we seemed to skim across the waves.

We made straight for the centre of the reef where the rocks were sharpest and tallest. I felt sure we must be sundered by the teeth of stone. I believe I may have uttered some kind of imprecation. I don't know to whom. Perhaps it was answered. More likely, the Ship of the Dead cannot be sunk by anything in our base world. In any case, we sailed right though the deadly rocks, dancing on the wild foam.

My fear made me oblivious to my surroundings. Only once we were in the quiet of the bay did I realise that the boat was becoming less and less distinct. The timbers beneath my hand were translucent as if they, too, like the long drowned, had finished with this world. The prow itself, though still substantial to my touch, appeared like paper, as if my hand could push through it into the cold black water beyond. The mast seemed no more than a blade of straw. The aft panels were quite invisible. At last, the beach approached. Now it was as if the two of us, the gaunt man and I, were hovering across the waves, so transparent had the boat become.

Just as it felt that my imagination could no longer sustain the image of the craft and I must drown, I felt myself thrown up onto the sand. I lay still for a moment, dazed with all I had seen. I was drenched from the spray. The waves lapped at my legs but I hadn't the strength to pull myself upright. Then I noticed the gaunt man already trudging away up the beach. The sun was rising and a pale shaft of yellow light illuminated his sunken features.

I dragged myself to my feet and ran after him. 'Why you?' I cried.

He held my gaze for a moment then replied, in a voice thick with sorrow and resignation:

'Because I was called.'

I let go of his arm and the man continued on his weary way. I watched him go. There was, in the awkward droop of his shoulders, a terrible lassitude – or at least so it seemed to me.

I thought again of the carved bones that dangled from the timbers of his roof – all the vile little faces. I pictured him in his lonely cabin, working away at some of that very evening's passengers. He carved them as they must have been in life, but I could not have done the same. I wondered if he was the only man allowed to see the men they had been. As an interloper or a stowaway, I had perceived the desperate transformations that death had wrought.

I knew that I would be haunted for ever by what I had seen. But how much worse must it be for he whose role was forever to transport the drowned into the next life? And, in recompense for this task not of his own choosing, to be ostracised by family, neighbour and friend.

I sank back down onto the sand. The sun was not yet warm but I allowed its brightness to banish the visions of the night from my consciousness. The waves lapped closer, I shielded my eyes and looked out at the island.

*

Some time later, the routine of the day in the village began again. The men dragged their boats down past me and put out to sea. The women brought wood for the fire. The two children brought me one of the earthenware jugs of fresh water and I thanked them and drank deeply. The other jug was emptied into the eternal broth and the children were dispatched to refill them.

Did they know what horrors I had endured during the night?

I stayed where I was until the sun was high in the sky, allowing the steady and timeless pace of the villagers going about their business to soothe my troubled spirit. Someone brought leaves for the pot. Someone else climbed the uncertain stair and returned a little later with a hessian bag of root vegetables – turnips, I thought, from a distance.

Finally, the fishing boats came back in with their catch, without mishap. I watched but, this time, did not assist as they were hauled up onto the sand. The fishermen tidied their nets and lines and prepared their catch for the cauldron.

I realised it was time for me to be gone. I did not belong here, however romantic my first associations had been. I returned to the small house where I had been so generously received and collected my things. I left a few coins on the table in recognition of their hospitality.

Outside, the sun was bright on the monument in the centre of the village. I paused a while, now understanding it did not commemorate a saint. The opposite, in fact. It was, rather,

Ankou. The fisherman called by name in the deep of the night to transport those lost to the sea to the world beyond.

At the base of the monument a small drift of loose sand had blown against the stone, forming a soft dune. I knelt and brushed it away, revealing an inscription. The stonemason had carved the letters in an angular style, almost like Celtic runes. It took me a moment to decipher their meaning. Eventually I solved the puzzle by tracing them with my finger. In this way I imparted to them a kind of cursive flow that put me in mind of my grandfather's old-fashioned handwriting. Indeed, no sooner was the memory of those days rekindled than I realised that I had known the name of the place all along: the Bay of the Departed.

I made my way to the stair and began to climb back up the cliff. I paused halfway and scanned the beach. I suppose the rhythm of life was the same each day in that place. I saw the gaunt villager cross the sand and watched as he disappeared among the rocks and pools at the northern end. No one paid him any attention. He was afforded no more respect than a shadow.

When I reached the fingerpost, with its three directions offered to the traveller, this time I took the path inland as most likely to lead me to a town where a train could transport me, as swiftly as technology would allow, back to the metropolis.

My journey was done.

Author's Note

This is the second of the stories inspired by Breton folklore. The westernmost tip of the Brittany coast, jutting out into the Atlantic Ocean, is alive with legends of the sea. Mythical creatures, giants, sprites, a kind of Dreamtime that explains the violence and the beauty of the coastline. The stories are often harsh and, to modern ears, cruel. Men and women destined to live out the same sacrifices for all of time, retribution for crimes committed by earlier generations or as an attempt to appease the angry sea.

My version of the Ankou is based on research and translation undertaken by my husband, Greg Mosse, from the books inherited from my uncle in April 2013. I chose to set the story in the period between World War I and World War II, where the way of life still followed the steady tread of the century before and the century before that, and aimed to capture a timelessness in the retelling of the old folk tale.

As in many ghostly stories, the narrator is an outsider who finds himself drawn into a strange, hidden community. Today, this part of Brittany is famous for its surfing and seafood. But the ancient legend – the one that has endured 'ever since the world began' – insists that the Baie de Trépassés, the Bay of the Departed, has always been a portal into death.

LA FILLE DE MÉLISANDE

Allemonde, a legendary land
The Past

Author's Note

This story was written in May 2008 for a 75th-anniversary celebration for Glyndebourne Opera House in Sussex, *Midsummer Nights*. Each author in the collection was invited to choose one – significant – opera as their inspiration and I chose *Pelléas et Mélisande* by Claude Debussy. Debussy is an off-stage character in the second of my Languedoc Trilogy, *Sepulchre*, which is partly set during the 1890s, so I had been listening to a great deal of French impressionist music and reading symbolist poetry, plays and novels to all the better immerse myself in the world of *fin-de-siècle* Paris.

Pelléas et Mélisande, the only opera Debussy wrote, premiered at the Opéra-Comique in Paris in April 1902. Adapted from Maeterlinck's symbolist play of the same name, it had mixed reviews at the time, though quickly became seen as marking a turning point in the development of opera from its nineteenth-century traditions to a musical form lighter on its feet.

For readers not familiar with Maeterlinck's tragic tale or Debussy's interpretation, here are the bare bones of the story. A man quick to anger, violent and jealous, Prince Golaud comes across a young woman, Mélisande, wandering lost in a forest. Timid, fearful, traumatised, she does not know where she has come from – though she remembers a sea journey – and has no idea why she finds herself in this strange, dark kingdom. Golaud marries her and takes her home to the court of his grandfather, the old blind King Arkel, where Golaud's mother Geneviève and his young son from an earlier marriage, Yniold, live. Golaud's half-brother, Pelléas, is also resident at the castle, though he is seeking permission from Arkel to leave.

This being opera, Pelléas and Mélisande fall in love. She is expecting Golaud's child, but she lives in fear of his violent temper and his jealousy – in Act I, when she loses her gold wedding ring, Golaud forces her to go to find it, despite her terror of the dark – so she looks, in part, to Pelléas for protection. Suspicious, vengeful, Golaud becomes obsessed with finding out the 'truth' – '*la verité*' – of the relationship between his half-brother and his wife, and he forces his son, Yniold, to spy on the pair. When Golaud sees them taking their leave of one another by the fountain in the grounds – they understand their love affair cannot be – he stabs Pelléas and pursues the grieving Mélisande. The closing scene of Act V sees Mélisande going into labour prematurely and dying as her daughter is born, without ever holding her. Even then, rather than seeking forgiveness or attempting to atone for his actions, Golaud still demands 'the truth'. The whispering final lines hint that the same fatalistic pattern of misery and twisted love is destined to continue down the generations.

From there, I imagined the childhood of this unwanted, un-mothered child, Mélisande's daughter – I gave her the name Miette, 'little one' – and what might it have been like to grow up in the sombre halls of the castle, in the shadow of murder. How Miette might have felt hearing rumours about her mother's death and her uncle's murder, her suspicions of what might have happened to Yniold's mother, Golaud's first wife. Seeing her father not brought to account for his deeds, because of his high birth, yet nonetheless a man haunted by the past and making an annual pilgrimage to the scene of his crime. With such a background, it seemed natural that Miette, purposeful and determined, would grow up to want to avenge her mother.

In the writing, I wanted to mirror the dreamy, otherworld quality of Debussy's score, the indeterminate setting, the blurring of past and present and future, the sense that nothing was certain, nothing was quite as it seemed. Such is the nature of mythologies and legend, both symbolic and real, not fixed in place or time, but rooted instead in impression, in emotion, in atmosphere. My story is set, however, on the occasion of Miette's eighteenth birthday . . .

La Fille de Mélisande

> The ideal would be two associated dreams.
> No time, no place.
>
> CLAUDE DEBUSSY,
writing about Pelléas et Mélisande in 1890

White is the colour of remembrance. The hoar frost on the blades of grass that cling to the castle walls, the hollow between the ribs and the heart. A shroud, a winding sheet, a ghost.

Absence.

The trees are silhouettes, mute sentinels, slipping from green to grey to black in the twilight. The forest holds its secrets.

Mélisande's daughter, Miette, presses herself deeper into the green shadows of the wood. She can see glimpses of *La Fontaine des Aveugles* through the twisted undergrowth and juniper bushes. It is late in the day and already the light has fled the sombre alleyways of the park and the gloomy tracks that cross the forest like veins on an old man's hands.

*

White is the colour of grief.

This is the anniversary of her mother's death when, according to the mythology of the land, the paths between one world and the next are said to be open. It is not a night to be abroad. It is also Miette's birthday, although this has passed without celebration or comment these past eighteen years. The date has never been marked by feasts or fanfares or ribbons.

The story of Mélisande – forbidden love, tragic beauty, a heroine dead before her time – this is the architecture of legend, of fairytale, of poetry and ballad. How could the existence of an unwanted, though resilient, daughter possibly compare? A watchful daughter biding her time.

Miette presses her hand against the silk of her robe, feeling the reassuring crackle of the paper. It is her testament, her confession, an explanation of the act she intends to carry out today. She knows her father, Golaud, has murdered once, if not twice – and holds him responsible for her mother's death – but yet he has kept his liberty. He has never been called to account. This is not how it will be for her. Although she is the great-granddaughter of old King Arkel, she is a girl not a boy. She is considered of no account. Besides, Miette wants to explain her deeds, make herself understood. In this, as in so many other ways, she is not her mother's daughter. Everything about Mélisande's life – her delicate spirit, her fragile history – remains as indistinct as a reflection moving upon the surface of the water. Where had she come from before Golaud found her and brought her to Allemonde? What early grief had cracked her spirit? What were her thoughts as her wedding ring fell, twisting, down into the well, knowing the loss of it would matter so much? How tripped her heart when she looked at Pelléas and saw her love reflected in his eyes? Did she catch her breath? Did he?

Did she know, even then, that her story would be denied a happy ending?

Miette grew up in the shadow of these stories, now grown stale and battered around the edges. Whisperings about her father, Golaud, and his violent jealousy. Of her mother, Mélisande, and her gentleness. Of how her long hair tumbled down from the window like a skein of silk. Of her uncle, Pelléas, and his folly. Of the others who stood by and did nothing.

*

Green is the colour of history.

Not the white and black of words on a page or notes on a stave. Not the frozen grey of tombstones and chapels. It is green that is the colour of time passing. Olive moss, sable in places, covering the crow's feet cracks in the wall. Emerald weeds that spring up on a path long unused. The lichen covering, year by timeless year, the inscription on the headstone, the letters, the remembered name.

At her nurse's knee, Miette learned the history of Pelléas and Mélisande. A history, a tale, is no substitute for a mother, but it gives a purpose to the suffering. Their story is the legend of Allemonde, a tale perfect in its construction – *un amour défendu*, a sword raised in anger. Always the balance of the light with the dark, the ocean with the confines of the forest, the castle and the tower. The colours, the texture of the story, Miette pieced together from what was left unsaid between her half-brother, Yniold, and her father.

The truth she learned from her grandmother, Geneviève. Of how men use women ill. How money buys safety, if not peace.

Of how the faults of one generation are passed down, silent and sly, to the next. Of how the truth is always shabby, always mundane when set next to the stuff of legend.

In her green hiding place in the forest, Miette sighs, caught between boredom and terror. Her confession and weapon lie concealed beneath her cloak. She is eighteen today. She will act, today.

Il est presque l'heure.

Her father's custom on this day are well known. From the white-haired beggars at the gate to the servants that walk the sombre corridors of the castle, all of Allemonde knows how Golaud, the widower — some say, the murderer of wives — makes his annual pilgrimage to *La Fontaine des Aveugles* on the anniversary of Mélisande's death, though Miette's birthday is not remembered. Golaud comes to mourn, some say, or to pray. To weep, to pick over the bones of his life. No one knows if it is remorse or grief that guides his steps. He has never shared that chapter of his story and Miette never asked for fear it would strip her purpose from her.

In the distance, the chiming of the bell. The sheep in the fields begin their twilight chorus, the mournful chorus for the passing of the day. Out at sea, the sun is sinking slowly down beyond the horizon, as every day for centuries. And in the palace, the slow and steady business of lighting the candles will now begin. The yellow flames dancing up along the stone walls and grey corridors.

The legend of Mélisande holds that she dreaded the dusk. Miette does not know if this is true. They say that Mélisande feared the night. The ringing of the Angelus bell, the closing of the gates in a rattle of wood and metal and chain — all this made her think of the grave where the worms and spiders dwelt. Mélisande turned to the west, or so Miette's nurse told her, to the setting sun and the shore, as if looking for that first ship, long departed, which had brought her as a child-bride to Allemonde from who knows where. As if hearing, still, the cries of the sailors and the gulls. An echo of a memory of happier times? Miette glances down and sees the tips of her satin slippers are stained with the first touches of the evening dew brushing the grass.

She shivers and pulls her cloak tight around her with her slim, strong arms. Deep in the folds of cloth, she presses the tip of the knife against her thumb, softly at first, then harder until her skin is pierced, then withdraws her hand. A single, red pearl of blood hangs suspended, like a jewel in the twilight.

There are beads of perspiration at the nape of her neck now beneath the canopy of her hair, worn long in remembrance of her mother. The mother who never held her. Although an inconvenience, the braids are a symbol of the connection between them. Brushed, plaited, smoothed. Though everyone tells Miette she is more her father's daughter. She is quick to temper, black moods threatening, easily frustrated.

Vengeful.

Beneath the trees, Miette shifts slightly from foot to foot, feeling the cold seeping up from the earth and the roots into her young bones. She does not know how long she has been waiting, entombed in the green embrace of the wood. Long enough for dusk to fall, it seems both an eternity and a moment. Eighteen years, in truth, and although she has been biding her time, all these minutes and hours and weeks, Miette feels panic rising in her throat, nausea, sour and bitter. She wills herself not to lose her nerve. Not now, not at the moment she has been planning for so long. Waiting for.

Pas maintenant.

*

Red is the colour of dying. What else could it be?

The violent rays of the setting sun through glass, flooding the chamber crimson. The petals pulled from a rose, strewn on the cobbled stones of a garden no longer tended. The colour of the damaged struggling heart. Blood dripping through the fingers.

To steady her nerves, Miette sends her thoughts flying back to the castle. She remembers herself at seven or eight years old, carried on Yniold's shoulders. Laughing, sometimes. Content, sometimes. But, quick, the darker memories come. Her past unfolds in her memory like the decaying slats of a paper fan. Older, eleven or twelve, tiptoeing alone down dusty corridors. Or, later still, hidden beneath the covers in her cold chamber, hands over her ears, trying not to hear her father shouting or Yniold weeping. Fear or humiliation, the sound was the same.

A bird flies up out of the trees, the abrupt beating of its wings upon the air mirroring the rhythms of her own anxious pulse. Miette narrows her eyes, sharpens her ears. In the distance, now, she can hear something. The subtle snap of twigs on the path, the rattling of rabbits seeking cover in the undergrowth, the shifting of the atmosphere. Someone is coming.

Him? The man who is her father, though she feels no love or duty to him? Is it he?

Miette stiffens. She has imagined this scene so many times. The single strike of the knife, an act of revenge. An eye for an eye, a blade for a blade. She has imagined how Golaud, wounded, would reach out his hands to her, as once Mélisande had reached for the baby daughter she could not hold. How he would ask her forgiveness.

And, even now, she could give it. Absolve him for his sins. Absolve herself for what she has done.

'*Je te pardonne. Je te pardonne tout.*'

That hour has not yet come. Miette waits, holding her breath, wishing the deed could be over. Or need not to be done at all.

The light from a lantern, jagged and uneven, is getting closer. Miette can distinguish the sound of breathing above the twilight sighings and whisperings and chitterings of the forest. The rattle of an old man's chest as Golaud walks out of the darkness, out of the cover of the trees and into the glade, following the well-worn path to *La Fontaine des Aveugles* – the Fountain of the Blind Men – to the place where Pelléas fell.

He moves slowly, pain in every step. Miette watches him and feels nothing. His body is failing him. He is old. His wounds, from war or the hunt, sing loud in the damp evening air. The scars, beneath the velvet of his robes, remind of hunting accidents and the memory of metal and spear. The crumbling of sinew and bone, eating him away from the inside out, grief or regret or anger? For eighteen years she has asked herself the same question, and received no answer. But she does not pity him. She cannot. She thinks only that he must be called to account. In Yniold's absence, his lack of will, it falls to her.

A daughter to avenge a mother, a less familiar story.

Golaud places the lantern uncertainly on the edge of the well. Miette waits. It is not yet her turn to step upon the stage. Her father is muttering, talking, but so softly that she cannot distinguish one word from the next. She moves a little closer, picks out the words.

'*La vérité. La vérité.*'

Over and over, like a chorus refrain, the syllables bleeding one into the other and back again. Demanding the truth. The words he said to his Mélisande as she lay dying.

Tell me the truth.

Golaud leans forward, two twisted hands in the yellow halo of light on the grey stone of the well. Miette steps forward, in silence and without drama. For if she is to rewrite this story, it cannot be told in noise and emotion, but rather enacted with cold purpose. It is a practical ending, not a theatrical one.

One step forward, then two. *Un, deux, trois loup.* Coming to get you, Mr Wolf, ready or not. A game of grandmother's footsteps played by two lonely children, she and Yniold, in a desolate palace long ago.

With a third silent step, she is on him.

Now, at last, she is ready to join herself to him. A murderer for a father, a murderer for a daughter.

As Golaud stoops forward to gaze into the blind eye of the water, Miette has the advantage of height. Thinking of Mélisande and her Pelléas, of Yniold's mother too – dead before her time – Miette lifts the knife and, with the strength of both hands and the weight of her body, she brings the blade down between her father's shoulders.

He cries out, once, like an animal caught fast in the metal jaws of a trap, then nothing. She has heard it said that the soul takes flight alone and in silence. She does not know if this is true, only that he does not speak or cry out again.

Miette relinquishes her hold on the hilt and steps back, half stumbling on the hem of her cloak beneath her heel, sodden with dew. She, too, is silent. There is nothing to say, though she wills him to turn, wishing her act of vengeance to be understood. At the same time, she does not want to see the life leaving him or her own image reflected in his dying eyes.

Golaud falls forward, as once Pelléas had fallen. His hands slip from the wall, empty fingers scratching down the stone surface of the well, down to the ground. No crash of cymbals to mark the moment of death, no crescendo, merely justice done.

Then, a nightjar calls, a spur to action. Taking the letter from her pocket, Miette places it upon her father's body. The testimony of Mélisande's daughter, eighteen years in the telling. A confession of why and how she killed her father.

'*La vérité*,' she whispers.

This is the truth. Set it down, set it down.

The truth is that stories can be rewritten. Acts of love and death.

Miette stretches to take Golaud's lantern from the rim of the well, taking care not to touch him, then turns to walk back through the forest. How easy, it seems, to kill a man. So easy to separate the spirit from the skin and bone?

In the distance, the bell strikes another hour. It marks the end of one history and the beginning of another.

*

Gold is the colour of loyalty. Of a duty fulfilled.

THE REVENANT

The Fishbourne Marshes, Sussex

Winter 1955

The Revenant

When latest autumn spreads her evening veil,
And the grey mists from these dim waves arise,
I love to listen to the hollow sighs
Thro' the half leafless wood that breathes the gale.
For at such hours the shadowy phantom pale,
Oft seems to fleet before the poet's eyes;
Strange sounds are heard, and mournful melodies
As of night wanderers who their woes bewail!

from Sonnet XXXII, 'To Melancholy'
CHARLOTTE TURNER SMITH

I first saw her on a Thursday afternoon. She was ahead of me on the path out on the marshes, walking fast as if to keep an appointment. Her hands were dug deep in her pockets and her shoulders hunched. A blue belted jacket and pleated skirt, white shirt just showing above the collar and shoes suitable for pavements not mud. Seamed stockings. Later, I realised why she looked familiar and why the look of her struck a false note.

But not then. Not that first time.

*

That Thursday, I stopped, puzzled I'd not noticed her before. The path, at this point, was narrow and accessed only from Mill Lane, and though I usually walked down to the estuary in the afternoon, when I could get away, it wasn't a popular spot. Although the lights of the lending library were visible on the far side of the field, most local people considered this area west of the Mill Pond too deserted, too overgrown and that November it had rained and rained.

She was too far ahead for me to make out her features and, besides, she didn't turn round. But her brown hair, visible beneath the rim of her cap, looked salon curled and from the way she moved, I thought she was about my age. That, too, stuck in my mind. Those who did come out this way were mostly old men with time on their hands, or farm workers taking a short cut across the fields to the big houses up along. Not girls in their twenties.

I followed her along the path, in that awkward proximity of strangers. I picked up my pace, feeling my gumboots slip on the mud. Was I hoping to catch up with her? I'm not sure of anything except that she stayed precisely the same distance ahead. But when I rounded the bend in the path, she'd vanished. I stopped again, trying to work out where she'd gone. There was a trail that cut down through the reed mace to the water's edge, white stones marking a route over the mud flats at low tide. The sea was right up, though, and not even a local would reckon you could get across. I looked behind me, in case she'd doubled back, but there was no sign of her.

What else? An odd smell, like rotten eggs, like seaweed on the shore in summer.

*

Thursday, 24th November, 1955, an afternoon like any other. My routine, in those days, rarely altered. On Monday and Thursday afternoons, I helped out in the library as a volunteer. It was a debt, of sorts. When I was growing up in Fishbourne, the library was the only place I felt was mine. We had no books to speak of at home and, besides, my stepfather didn't think girls should waste time reading. Didn't think they were good for anything but cooking and fetching and carrying. In the library I was let alone. No one shouted at me, nobody took the mickey. Sitting cross-legged on the floor, I travelled the world in the company of Agatha Christie and Eleanor Burford and Rider Haggard, dreaming of what I'd be when I grew up. Nothing came of any of it – Harry's trouble with the police, then the war put paid to dreams of leaving – I retained an affection for the place. So when I found myself back in Fishbourne fifteen years later, the library seemed the obvious place to offer my services. And even now, when I stepped through the big oak doors, and breathed in the familiar perfume of dust and polish, life didn't seem so bad for an hour or two.

That Thursday the library was closed. A burst pipe had flooded Natural Sciences and we had all been sent home. So after I'd cleared the table and the dishes were stacked and drying on the draining board, I asked our neighbour, Mrs Sadler – who came in to keep an eye on my stepfather when I was at work – if she wouldn't mind staying on for a while anyway, so I could slip off.

I went out by the side door, turning the handle slowly so as not to disturb him. Old habits die hard. Over the main road, quiet in the drowsy part of the afternoon, down Mill Lane and out onto the estuary, where the salt marshes lay spread out like a battered old map. When we were children, my older brother forced me to climb down the bank into the muddy creek. I was scared of the filthy, tidal water, but I was more frightened of Harry's temper, so always did what he told me. It was different when I managed to get out on my own. Then, I could kick my heels. Bright days when the sun bathed the Downs in the distance in a chill yellow light. Stormy days when black clouds scudded along the horizon, the smell of bonfires heavy in the air. The soft days of spring, when pink ragged robin and southern marsh orchids pricked the green, or the white flowers of lady's smock, identified from the Collins Guide borrowed from the Natural History section in the pocket of my regulation school coat.

We left Fishbourne when I was twelve, too young to understand the whispers or the way neighbours fell silent when Harry stepped into the Woolpack Inn. I knew there was talk – about him, and my stepfather too – but my mother never explained and I was too timid a girl to ask. Then Harry signed up – moment he could, couldn't wait to get away – and went to war. Never came back. When we came back to Fishbourne, I realised there had been rumours about the pair of them, Harry and my stepfather, even before it happened. I never wanted to come back to this corner of Sussex – it rubbed it in how little I'd made of my life, to end up back where I'd started and been so unhappy – but my stepfather was insistent and my opinion wasn't taken into account. I understand now that, as his mind started to unravel, something drew him back.

These days there was a footbridge over the creek. Sometimes I stopped there a while, the wooden handrail greasy beneath my fingers, and told myself that, despite it all, things were better now. Pretended that time and the war had buried the past.

Wiped the slate clean.

*

For the last week of November, my stepfather's health kept me indoors. I couldn't go to work, couldn't even get out to the shops. We were locked together, he and I. One of those things. I'd always been scared of him, and he'd never shown any affection for me, but now Mum was gone it fell to me to look after him. Duty, just the way it was. There was no one else. So it wasn't until the following Thursday, December 1st, that I went back to the marshes.

I changed into my boots as I left the library, wrapped my indoor shoes in brown paper and put them in my handbag, then set off along the same path. It was a blustery day and the gulls were shrieking out at sea. Only as I got out onto the marshes did I realise I'd been half looking out for the girl I'd seen the week before. I suppose I'd been hoping we might talk. All the women my own age were married and had children or husbands to keep them occupied. The neighbours were nice enough, to pass the time of day with in the post office or the shop, but I had no friends. I kept hoping, but there was no sign of her and, as I climbed up to the flint sea wall, I had a knot of disappointment in my stomach.

Just someone to talk to.

*

That afternoon, I walked all the way to Oak Pond, where an old rowing boat lay abandoned in the silted water, and the trees hung low. I smoked a cigarette and thought about some domestic worry or another, before turning back. I'd been gone longer than usual and so I hurried, knowing Mrs Sadler would be ready with her lips pursed and her hat and coat at the door. Four o'clock. I remember glancing at my wristwatch.

Then, on the far side of the silent expanse of water, I saw something flash. At first, I thought it was the library, but realised it was too far over for that. A light, right out in the middle of the marshes where Cornmill House had been. In Victorian times there had been several mills on the eastern side of Fishbourne Creek, powered by wind or by the sea, though they were mostly gone now. The water cornmill and the house attached had all but burned down during the First World War and the high tides each spring had done the rest. Its black and rotting features had been a childhood landmark, a draw for brave or foolish boys to explore.

By the time we were back in Fishbourne, it had gone. Pulled down last year, Mrs Sadler had told me. After fifteen years, it still attracted too many gawpers, too many ghouls. A shrine, of sorts. And I remembered back to how newspaper reports at the time claimed Cornmill House was being used as a rendezvous long before it became notorious. Smugglers evading the excise men, ghosts, enemy spies. It was another occasion I'd taken refuge in the library, poring over a local history book and mugging up. Drawings, maps of underground passages, rumours, I knew the history of the house backwards though I'd never been inside. My brother Harry boasted he and his friends used to go in, dare each other to stay all night. Seen writing on the walls and blood on the stairs, he'd said, smears on the glass where smugglers had kept their prisoners in the old days.

At first, I thought he was making it up to scare me. I didn't believe him. Later, when the police came, he denied he had ever been there. He'd only been home on leave for a few days, he said. A few pints in the Woolpack, sleeping in a proper bed, no time. But as I listened through the crack in the door and heard him wriggle like a fish on the line, I knew for certain he had been in the house at some time or another and knew the worst it had to tell. I told no one. No one asked me anyway. Harry rejoined his unit and was posted to France. His luck ran out. When he died a couple of weeks later, his secret died with him.

Another flash, bright, gone, then another. I pulled my coat tight around me. There should not have been a light there. Another flash. A signal of some kind? The sight of it, on that cold December dusk, and the past fifteen years fell away and I was back there again in our old kitchen, with the fug from the stove and the condensation on the inside of the windows. My mother's worn, housewife's red hands twisting at her pinny and the look of calculation in my stepfather's eyes as the copper questioned Harry.

I took a deep breath, in, then out. No sense in raking it all up again. That house was gone. Harry was gone, Mum too. My stepfather no longer knew who he was. And if I had seen a light where Cornmill House used to be – and already I was no longer sure – odds on it was only someone carrying a lantern over the fields to Apuldram or to the church. Nothing iffy about it.

*

All the same, I looked for the book in the library the following Monday, but it had been taken out of circulation and there was nothing else in the Local History section that caught my fancy. Besides, it was ever so busy. I had no time to think about the light on the marshes or Cornmill House. We put up the

Christmas decorations. Children from the village school came to sing carols around the tree. We made paper chains.

The nights were bad that week, though. My stepfather woke two or three times between midnight and six. A bad conscience, Mrs Sadler said, when I told her. So by the time the next Thursday came around, I was tired to my bones and tempted to go straight home from work. But, telling myself the fresh air would do me good, I set off once more along the path. A mist had come in from the sea and everything was muffled, suspended, though I could hear the suck of the tide and the call of black-headed gulls massing in the harbour. It was cold, proper December weather, and the chill seemed to soak through my woollen hat and mittens.

I'd barely gone a few steps when I noticed the smell again, the same as a fortnight ago, though far stronger. A foul stench of rotting seaweed and mud and rust. As if something in the earth had been turned inside out. I took a few more steps, then heard something moving in the reeds alongside the path. Not a noise quite, more a shifting of the air. Though I told myself not to be silly, the nerves twisted in my stomach.

I walked faster. The sound kept pace with me, a kind of rattling, shimmering, in the rushes to my left, then a loud crack of the reed stems underfoot, as if someone was pushing their way through towards the path. I felt a moment of blind panic, not sure where the sound was really coming from or whether it was just my imagination playing tricks on me.

I forced myself to stop. Stood still, completely still. Now, hearing nothing. The noise had stopped and yet, I knew, without a shadow of a doubt, that someone was close by. I could feel it in the pricking of my skin. Hands clenched inside my mittens, my palms greasy with fear, slowly I turned round. All the way round, 360 degrees, eyes staring into the white fog, but not able to make anything out. I was torn between turning back or going on. I took a few snatched steps more, the rustling in the reed mace again, the stench even stronger now. Looking around me, behind me, panic rising crawling over the surface of my skin. Was someone following me? Was there someone out here on the deserted marshes, just waiting for a girl like me to venture out on her own?

Then, then.

Suddenly, ahead of me on the path, was a figure, come out of nowhere. Indistinct in the mist, blocking my way. My hand flew to my mouth, stifling a scream, then a moment of relief. I gasped. It was her, it was the same woman, dressed just the same as before.

'You didn't half give me . . .' I started to say, then I stopped. There was something not right in her silence and the way she was standing, her head down, hands hanging loose by her side.

'You gave . . .'

Then, all at once, I realised why she looked familiar. She was the spit of the girl who'd gone missing fifteen years ago. They'd run her photograph on the front page of the *Observer* for weeks. And, more to the point, she was wearing the same WAAF uniform – blue jacket, shirt and tie, pleated skirt, cap. Women's Auxiliary Air Force girls, they'd been billeted all over the village during the war.

I couldn't help myself. My eyes slipped down to her hands. I saw her gloves were torn, fragments of pale material, all in tatters at the cuffs. A matching scarf around her neck, pale pink with a red lining, coming unravelled too. No, not gloves.

Not gloves, but skin. Torn, tattered skin.

A wave of nausea rose in my throat, threatening to choke

me. It wasn't possible. I took another step back, another, then turned and started to run. Stumbling, slipping, struggling to keep on my feet, running back along the path. I could feel her dead eyes on my back, felt the stench of seaweed and rotten eggs all around me, a palpable living thing, catching in my nose and my mouth. My legs moved faster, running through the reed mace, trying to outrun whatever was behind me.

Salt Mill House loomed suddenly up out of the mist. Was I safe? For a fleeting instant, I considered banging on the door and asking for help. But, then, what would I say? That I'd seen a girl on the path and got the wind up? And the foul smell hung about me, on my clothes, my hair, seeping through my skin, and I couldn't stop. Didn't dare stop.

I was out on the mudflats now, treacherous in the dusk. My boots sank lower at each step. The mud was like clawing hands around my ankles, trying to drag me down. Out here, pockets of swamp lay concealed amongst the reeds, sinking mud and false land where a person could be pulled down into the estuary. Flecks of grass, of seaweed, of sludge splattered up onto the back of my legs and skirt and hem of my coat. My throat was sore from running, burning like a slug of whisky in a child's mouth, but panic kept me going, deeper into the marsh. On across the eel grass, where the savannah sparrows nested, over the samphire, faded at the tail of the year, past the creek, until finally Mill Lane was in sight and the solid, familiar outline of the library. My refuge then, a refuge now.

I stopped running, put my hand against the familiar bricks, to catch my breath. At last, I turned and looked behind me. Nothing was there, no one. I realised the smell had gone and the mist, too, was beginning to lift.

I don't know how long I stood there, only that already

embarrassment was replacing fear. How easily I'd let my imagination get the better of me. I'd been hoping to run into her, then, when I did, I turned tail like a rabbit. The girl herself, whoever she was, what must she think? She'd think I was off my rocker. So what if she was dressed in rather old-fashioned clothes? And as for the marks on her wrists, just a trick of the light in the fading afternoon. She'd hardly have been walking around otherwise, would she?

I hesitated a moment outside. I was late home already and I looked a sketch. Salt water splashed up the back of my raincoat, my gloves stiff with mud. Mrs Sadler would be sure to pass comment, she was the type who didn't let anything go. But there was something I had to do, read, before I went home. I wouldn't rest else. Mrs Sadler would have to wait.

I ran up the steps and into the library. To my relief, Albert was still on the front desk, his glasses perched on the tip of his red nose. Saying I'd forgotten something, and he wasn't to worry, I headed through the stacks to the archive room at the back of the building, where back issues of local and parish newspapers were kept. Floor-to-ceiling hanging files and oversize drawers, nothing had been put onto film yet. In the middle there was a large central desk with drawers, large enough to accommodate ten people working at any one time. I scanned the years, months, weeks, until I found the box I wanted:

NOVEMBER 1940

My heart going nineteen to the dozen, I flicked through until I found the edition I was after. Saw what I didn't want to see. I stared at the black and white photograph in the newspaper, looking into the eyes of the murdered girl. Her hair curled out beneath the cap, the belted jacket and pleated skirt, shirt and tie. I caught my breath. And beneath, the description of the murder: her throat cut and marks on wrists suggesting she'd been kept captive for a while before her body was found in Cornmill House.

I slumped down on the chair, the photograph bringing it all back. The whispers, the pointed fingers, the speculation. Remembering when the police had gone, hearing Mum and my stepfather arguing in whispers, so the neighbours wouldn't hear through the walls. She took Harry's side, of course. Tried to defend him. Said they were talking to every man over sixteen, nothing sinister about it. Bound to be one of the soldiers billeted at Oakwood or Goodwood. Besides, what respectable girl would go on her own, to a place like that? Asking for trouble.

I put the newspaper back in the box and the box back in the stacks, then turned off the light. I waved to Bert on the way out and held up my bag, proof that I'd found what I was looking for, then I went out into the fading afternoon. Cold, dark, ice underfoot. Proper December weather. Back up Mill Lane, over the road to the row of terraced cottages where we lived. The back door was unlocked. I took off my boots and hung my coat, inside out, on the back of the door, before calling out.

'It's only me,' I said, going through to the hall. 'Sorry I'm late. I got held up.'

Mrs Sadler was dressed for outside, hat and gloves on, hands folded in front of her. She glanced pointedly at the clock on the window sill by the sink.

'How's he been?'

'Same as usual,' she said in a tight, clipped voice.

'Has he had his tea?'

'At four. He's asleep now.' Her voice was begrudging, hard

done by. 'He's been agitated all afternoon, mind you. Talking about some girl. Your brother Harry, too, though it's hard to know what he's saying. The language.'

'I'm sorry if he's offended you, Mrs Sadler,' I said, more sharply than I intended. 'Thanks for staying on. I'll see you Monday, as usual?'

A sly look crossed her broad face. 'I don't know. Mr Sadler doesn't like me coming here, you know. He's not one for talk.'

I was tempted to say, no I didn't know, to make her come out with it. Admit that she'd heard the rumours about my stepfather, about our family. At least then I could say something in our defence. But I was more shaken up than I cared to admit and, besides, who else would come in and sit with him? So I just suggested we should perhaps come to a new financial arrangement, to compensate for any inconvenience. I got a note out and put it on the table. Would that help matters indoors? I could see her thinking about it, totting up the extra few bob. She held out a moment longer, then reached and pocketed the ten shillings.

'See you Monday,' she said.

*

After she'd left, I locked the back door and since there was no one about to see, stepped out of my skirt and sponged the mud as best I could. While it dried, I put on my old gardening skirt that was hanging over the back of the chair where I'd been mending it earlier. I looked at the clock. Five o'clock and it was pitch black. The idea of the long evening ahead was almost more than I could bear, but I knew I'd get on with it just the same. Just as I always did.

I leaned over the sink and pulled on the curtains to shut out the dark. The wire was old and the fabric too heavy, so they stuck halfway, as they usually did, leaving a slat of silver coming in from the light in the alley that ran along the back of the cottages. I knew I should go in to the front room and see how he was, but I couldn't face it. I was still turning the events of the afternoon over in my mind.

Taking a tin of soup from the larder, I put a saucepan on the stove, cut a couple of slices of bread and buttered them, then put two pieces of cheddar on the side of our plates. All the time, turning over what had happened in my mind. I didn't come to any firm conclusion either way – had I seen someone at all or just imagined it? – only that I would steer clear of the marshes for the time being.

*

We ate our meal in silence. The hours crept by. I put on the wireless to keep him company and picked up the novel I'd been reading, *Marjorie Morningstar*. Set in 1930s America, about a girl who wants to be an actress, I'd liked the sound of it so much I'd bought a copy, rather than waiting for the library to get it in, but tonight it didn't hold my attention. My stepfather was restless, talking as he drifted in and out of sleep.

As I glanced over at his ruined face, I wondered at how I'd once been so scared of him. He'd been a big man in his day, working at the Anglesey Arms in Halnaker after we'd moved from Fishbourne, until that job, like all the others, fell through. Every time, he called them 'misunderstandings', said everyone was out to get him, but the plain truth was he was a drunk. After that last dismissal, he never worked again. He just sat about the house with a bottle in one hand, cigarette in the other, picking fights with any of us stupid enough to get in his way. Now, he hardly knew who he was. Thin as a rake, hardly able to speak or see, too frail to stand unaided.

Only me left now. Only him and me.

*

At nine o'clock, I began the business of getting him to bed. He slept down here now, to save him the stairs, but it still took a good half-hour to undress him, put him in his pyjamas, get him settled.

Once he was sorted out, I went back to the front room to get things straight for the morning, as if it mattered. Nobody but Mrs Sadler and the vicar ever visited. I turned off the table lamp, then walked through to the kitchen to get a glass of water. Except for the corridor of light coming in through the gap in the curtains, the room was dark. The cold tap spluttered, the pipes complaining, so I let it run a moment.

Then, out of the corner of my eye, I saw something move in the yard. A shadow, or reflection, I couldn't say. My stomach lurched. I put down the glass on the draining board, the water slopping over the side, and peered out. Nothing. Not a cat, not a soul about, nothing. I knew I'd locked the back door earlier, but I checked again, just to be sure. The key, which I always left in the lock, was gone.

I crouched down and ran my fingers over the coarse mat and was absurdly relieved when my fingers connected with the cold metal. Silly to get the wind up. I shot the bolts top and bottom, just to be sure. After the events of the day, my nerves were bad. I picked up my glass and headed out into the cold hallway, then stopped dead.

My stepfather was standing in the corridor. Somehow, without making a noise, he'd got himself up and out of bed on his own. My heart sank. It didn't happen often, but on the odd occasion when he did wake in the night, not knowing where he was, it could take hours to get him settled again.

'What are you doing up?' I said, not expecting an answer. 'You'll catch your death.'

He was rocking from side to side, old legs that could barely hold him. His hands were balled into fists. I felt a wave of revulsion, though I knew I ought to feel pity. Then I saw his eyes. They were sharp for the first time in years, unclouded, and fixed at a point behind me.

'She's here.'

His voice was thin, quavering, but the words were clear.

'What?' I blurted out, shocked that he'd spoken at all.

'She's here. Come for me.'

'Who's here?'

But even as I said it, of course I knew. I could feel the prickling on my skin at the back of my neck, my hands. And the smell of the shore at low tide. Seaweed and sulphur and mist, the foul breath of the grave. I didn't want to look round, but I couldn't stop myself. Taking my eyes off him, for a second, slowly I turned. To face the girl I knew was standing behind me. The skin at her wrists, rubbed raw where the wire had cut through. The ragged red seam where his knife had dragged across her throat, left to right. The work of a right-handed man. Not Harry. Harry was left-handed. For all his faults, not Harry.

For an instant, time seemed to stop and I saw her clearly, a terrible melding of both the girl she had been and the girl she now was, a girl fifteen years dead, lying in the churchyard with a headstone at her feet.

I wanted to speak, to reach out to her, but terror had stolen my voice from me. Then, slowly, she began to lift her head, the same steady and deliberate movement as on the path earlier. This time, I held my ground. Saw her brown eyes, determined face, the brown curled hair kissing her chin.

*

All at once a rush of air, cold and damp like the mist on the marshes, as if someone had opened a door and let the night in. And a dreadful howling, like a deer caught in a steel trap. For a split second, the girl appeared to smile as she gazed upon the face of the man who had murdered her. Then, before my eyes, her face began to change. Her features, pretty printed on the front page of the newspaper all those years ago, started to collapse in upon themselves. Her brown eyes became red, then rolling white, her rouged lips shrivelled to black, her skin turning to a spider's web of veins and sinew.

Suddenly, without warning, she leapt.

At the hour of his death, she had come to claim him. I screamed, beating the air with useless hands, trying to protect myself or him, I can't say. But he didn't resist. Her bloody, broken body seemed to cover him, bones and blood, taking him with her. His legs buckled and he fell forward, arms by his side, making no attempt to break his fall.

Then silence.

*

I sank to the ground, knees drawn up to my chin, oblivious to the blood seeping across the tiles and soaking into the hem of my skirt. I heard nothing, was aware of nothing, until someone started banging on the front door and I heard them calling my name.

Later, they told me it was the sound of my stepfather screaming that alerted the neighbours. That, and a strange smell of rotting seaweed permeating through the thin cottage walls.

The doctor said it was a heart attack. A blessing, he called it, that he went so fast. One minute here, the next, gone. The blood from where he'd hit his head. Just like that. But I understood now. I knew he had been dying for years. Rotting from the inside out.

Waiting, all that time, for her to return.

*

And what of me? I found, after all that, I was happy in Fishbourne, now I was at no one's beck and call. I stayed in the cottage, painted it top to toe, discovered I liked living on my own. Every spare minute I spent researching, checking every tiny detail, until I was ready to write about the case. A famous unsolved murder in November 1940, the brutal killing of a WAAF girl in Cornmill House. Cleared my brother's name. Although Harry was never charged, suspicion hung over him – over us all – rightly as it turned out. My mother had gone to her grave never knowing the truth.

Or had she? From time to time, I wonder.

In my own small way, I became quite well known. An interview in the *Observer* and a few talks to the WI. My book sits on the True Crime shelves in the library where I still work. The church warden at St Mary's tells me that people often come to leave flowers at the girl's grave.

And on winter nights, the lights still shine through the windows of the library and out across the marshes. A sanctuary for anyone who needs a place to go.

Author's Note

I grew up in the 1960s and 1970s in a small village, Fishbourne, in West Sussex. To the east, the spire of the cathedral dominates the landscape. To the west are the bigger towns of Portsmouth and, further still, Southampton. To the north, the folds of the Sussex Downs – the estates of West Dean and Goodwood, the remains of an Iron Age fort on the Trundle looking down to the estuary. There is a Roman palace in Fishbourne, a small nineteenth-century church (expanded from its medieval origins), the Old Toll House at the site of the Fishbourne turnpike as well as many older cottages and houses dating back hundreds of years. Looking back, I see this is where my earliest interest in history came, simply living in a place where it was so evident in day-to-day life.

More important, though, was what lies to the south – the sea. Not the yellow sands of West Wittering and Bognor Regis, but rather the muddy and tidal estuary of Fishbourne Creek. My sisters and I played at the Mill Pond, hid in the reed mace and high grasses that towered over our heads. When I was older, rather solitary by nature in those days, I'd take a book out to the old flint sea wall and sit reading in the sun. The names of the houses and buildings around the estuary reflected the former industry of this part of the creek – Salt Mill, the Corn Mill, Paper Mill – buildings that are all gone or converted into flats, which still speak of the working landscape. There was, however, no lending library in Fishbourne. That is a ghost of my own imagining.

When I came across the idea of a 'revenant' – a visible ghost, or animated corpse, believed to return from the grave to terrorise or take revenge on the living: often their murderer or someone who had done them wrong in life – the story started to take shape. In particular, the idea that derelict or vanished buildings haunt a landscape in the way that a spirit might haunt a person. The word 'revenant' comes from the Latin *revenans*, meaning 'returning'.

A version of this story first appeared in two instalments in *The Big Issue*, December 2009.

ON HARTING HILL

South Harting Village, West Sussex
October 1961

On Harting Hill

On such a night, when Air has loosed
Its guardian grasp on blood and brain,
Old terrors then of god or ghost
Creep from their caves to life again;

from 'Low Barometer'
ROBERT BRIDGES

Friday, 27th October, 1961. That afternoon, I was late getting away. A burst water main in Tolworth, and down to one lane in Kingston, meant the going was slow and the traffic was heavy. It had been mild, but in the last few days the weather had turned unsettled. There was a light drizzle and the road was slippery and wet. Leaves, fallen, on the pavements.

All the same, I was comfortable enough in my Morris Minor, the heating rattling on full, rime on the inside of the windscreen as I crept forward in a stream of cars leaving London by the old Portsmouth Road. I half listened to the news on the wireless: unrest in the Paris suburbs, the last British troops leaving Kuwait, another stand-off between Soviet and American tanks at Checkpoint Charlie. The traffic inched forward.

A friend from my school days had invited me to stay for the weekend. A few like-minded chaps, Bill said, all of them single or, like me, recently divorced. All very informal, he'd said. Country walks and a pub lunch, a few hands of cards. A round of golf on Sunday morning. I hadn't seen Bill for years, but the thought of a change of scene was welcome and I'd accepted. Now, what with the traffic, I was in two minds about whether I'd done the right thing.

'Traffic's always bad Fridays,' Bill said. 'All the weekenders choking up the road.'

'Adding to their number,' I'd said, and we'd both laughed in that slightly awkward way of friends who had once known each other well.

'That's it,' he said. 'Friday it is. I'll send directions. We're hard to find the first time.'

'Can I bring anything?'

'Just yourself,' he'd replied. 'Just yourself.'

I tell you this, and in such detail, so you understand there was nothing out of the ordinary. It was an unexceptional Friday afternoon, nothing to mark it out. I was regretting accepting Bill's invitation, in the way of those things, but I wasn't anxious beyond what you'd expect from a man intending to spend the weekend with strangers. I was in good spirits, good health and I'd been sleeping better over the past few weeks.

*

Once I was out of London, I had a clear run of it and the first hour or so passed uneventfully. Traffic started to thin out. One by one, the commuter husbands hurrying home to their wives. The grey afternoon sky turned pink at dusk, then an inky blue. On road signs, the names of unfamiliar villages, places I'd never heard of and would never visit. As I drove on and on, I thought of all the people I'd never meet, settling down for their supper. A closed up garage on the corner and rows of shops, street after anonymous street of modern new houses on the outskirts of towns.

I made good time. Even so, it already was past nine o'clock by the time I turned off the main road and started to make my way cross country. Bill had promised a scratch meal, since we were all arriving at different times, but I was worried about pitching up after everyone else. I decided I'd stop, if I could, to let him know I was running late.

I didn't have long to wait. In a village called South Harting, I found a telephone box. The red paint was chipped and, inside, an acrid smell of damp and ash, but the phone itself was working. I dialled the number, waited for the pips and Bill's voice, pushed the coin into the slot.

'My wife won't mind,' Bill said when I explained I was still a good half hour away. 'She'll put something by for you.'

'If you're sure.'

'You don't mind, do you?' he called out.

I imagined him cupping the receiver with his hand and his wife smiling and shaking her head. In the background, I could hear the raised voices of men who've had one over the eight.

'She doesn't mind,' Bill said again. 'We'll see you when we see you.'

I came out of the phone box and lit a cigarette. I lingered a while to shrug the stale smell off my clothes, tempted by the convivial lights in the White Hart, but I knew I should press on. I allowed myself to finish the cigarette though and stretched my legs. Turning my collar to the cold and damp,

I wrapped my scarf a little tighter around my neck, then walked up the High Street towards the church of St Mary and St Gabriel, then back on the opposite side of the road. The air was filled with the scent of coal fires and wood, wet earth and ploughed fields. Squares of light from kitchen windows, an untenanted schoolhouse, it seemed a quintessentially English village.

As I unlocked the car, a customer came out of the Ship Inn, on the corner. I gave him good evening and raised my hat. He looked at me through ale-drenched eyes, bleary with surprise or suspicion, before stumbling away into the night.

'Please yourself,' I muttered, a little put out.

I took off my scarf, then checked Bill's handwritten map again to be sure I had the directions clear in my mind: through South Harting on the Uppark Road, turn sharp left to follow the road up through the woods for a couple of miles. At the top of Harting Down, when the trees started to thin out, look out for a sign to Bill's village.

*

I drove past a sleeping row of workmen's cottages, aware of the dense woodland beyond the outskirts of Harting. Left and left again, my foot lifted from the accelerator on the bends. Fallen leaves, a patchwork of colours of burgundy and copper and gold, lit suddenly by the car's headlamps. Right and left again, then I was plunged into the utter blackness of the countryside. Abrupt, silent. I fixed my eyes ahead, trying not to notice how the long tall trunks of the high trees loomed over the road or the way the ground fell violently away to the left. The engine was straining as I changed down a gear, then down again.

I'm an ordinary man – no imagination, my ex-wife used to say, proudly at first, then later with disappointment – but as I drove on and up into the woods, it seemed to me the darkness took on a life of its own. It seemed to bend and twist and curl around the car. The gnarled exposed roots of trees were the knuckles of an old man's hand and the trunks transformed themselves into a marching army. The glint of sharp eyes in the undergrowth, a fox or a badger, vibrated with menace and spoke of something beyond any normal night-time creature. Every branch had a face, a shape, a living purpose.

It was getting colder too. Pockets of low cloud hung in the hollow spaces between the army of pines or floated across the road, as if pushed by some unseen hand. A light drizzle, cloud turning to mist, mist to fog. Faces, contours, eyes, fingers finding shape in the wall of white. Telling myself not to let my wits run away with me, I switched on my fog lamps. It made little difference. I still could see no more than six inches in front of me and the mist still seemed to be full of creatures. The hypnotic swish of the windscreen wipers, along with the rattle of the heater and the straining of the engine, was making me feel dizzy. I swallowed, aware my mouth was dry. Right, then right again, following the turn of the road. Second gear, down to first in places as the track went winding and twisting this way and that. Left, then left again. Another tight bend, the endlessness of the surrounding woodland, another half-formed face staring hollow out of the mist, except this time it was real.

I slammed on the brakes.

'No!'

Did I shout out a warning or only in my head? I don't know, only that this time there really was a girl, not an apparition in the mist. Flesh and blood standing in the middle of the road and I was going to hit her. I stamped on the brake again, hands clenched, shoulders braced. The back wheels spun. Slipping, skidding, sliding towards the girl.

'Get out of the way!'

A thud of something beneath the car and I was thrown forward, hard against the steering wheel. After noise, silence. After movement, stillness. It took me a moment to realise the Morris Minor had come to a halt and I was still on the road, safe. Apart from a sharp pain in my ribs, I was all right.

What about the girl? Had I hit her?

I fumbled with the catch, my shaking fingers failing to get purchase, but in the end managed to fling open the door and stumble out into the night. I could barely see my hand in front of my face. But I called out, praying for an answer from another human voice.

'Where are you? Are you all right?'

The fog muffled everything, footsteps, twigs underfoot. I traced my way round the car, hand sliding across the metal so as not to lose my footing and go tumbling down, round to where I thought the girl had been standing. I crouched down to look under the car, dreading what I might see beneath the chassis, but there was nothing except a heavy branch caught in the front number plate.

My relief was short-lived. The ground fell steeply away, I could see that now. Had she tried to get out of the way and fallen down the wooded hillside? I called out again.

'Are you hurt?'

Then, suddenly, I saw her. Standing, silent, in a gap between the trees. Hardly visible in the mist, hardly there at all.

'What in God's name are you playing at?' Fear turned

swiftly to anger now I could see she was safe. 'Out here alone, at this time of night, you could have been killed.'

I saw how young she was, no more than seventeen or eighteen, and somehow that shocked me. Thin arms and legs, long drab hair framing a thin, pale face. A cheap dress with a narrow belt and rather old-fashioned shoes. Indoor shoes, not right for walking.

'You could have been killed.'

She stepped back, as if now only noticing me for the first time, and raised her head. Dark eyes, dark. No light in them.

'Yes,' she said. A quiet voice, barely audible.

'Well,' I said. She looked such a sorry little thing. I waited, thinking she'd explain why she was there or where she was going, but she said nothing more.

'Here,' I said, taking off my jacket and draping it over her thin shoulders. 'You're shaking. You're cold.'

She didn't thank me, merely stood there as if barely aware of the action or the weight of the material.

'Are you trying to get home? Did your lift let you down?'

She didn't look the type to have a boyfriend, but what did I know? I pulled the branch out from under the car.

'Well,' I said again. 'No harm done, I suppose.'

Although I wanted to press on, I knew Bill wouldn't worry and I couldn't leave her.

'You'd better let me drop you home,' I said. 'Where do you live, nearby? Harting?'

'Yes,' she said.

'Harting it is,' I said, hoping the car would start. 'I'm Tom, by the way. And you?'

At first, I thought she wasn't going to answer. Then, softly, she did.

'Mary. Mary Starr.'

'Pretty name,' I said, more to fill the silence than anything else. 'Come on then.'

*

With surprising speed, Mary seated herself behind me. I was conscious of her dark eyes on the back of my head as I found reverse and turned to go back down the hill. She didn't make a sound. I glanced at her in my driving mirror.

'Won't be long,' I said.

It was cold inside the car and I fiddled with the dial on the heater, but it didn't seem to be working. I could feel the weight of her sadness pressing down on me too. I wished the whole business was over and I was sitting in Bill's brightly lit sitting room with a whisky in one hand and a cigarette in the other.

'Smoke?'

Mary gave no sign she'd heard me.

'You won't mind if I do?'

I shrugged and lit a cigarette anyway.

*

The drizzle had stopped and there was no fog at the bottom of the hill, but I was relieved all the same when I saw the lights at the edge of the village. I glanced again in the mirror. Mary was still, motionless, fingers twisting the shabby material of her dress, swamped by my jacket. I drove past the church, with its copper spire, past the houses, waiting for her to give me directions to where she lived. I was forced to brake as a fox shot across the High Street in front of us.

'Will this do?'

When she still didn't answer, I pulled over by the telephone box, where I'd parked earlier, killed the engine and twisted round in my seat.

She wasn't there. The car was empty.

I got out, at that moment more annoyed about my jacket than worried about the girl.

'Mary?' I called out to the empty street.

*

I strode into the Ship Inn, determined to find out where Mary's family lived. After everything I'd done for her, I wasn't inclined to let it go. It wasn't just the jacket, but my wallet and pocket diary too.

'Anyone know where the Starr family lives?'

Again, is it memory playing tricks that recalls an intake of breath in the public bar, the sharp glances crossing from the landlord to the old men on the table beside the fire?

'It's Mary I'm after,' I said.

'Again,' someone muttered, but a glare from his companions silenced him and he hunched back into his beer.

'Ten yards up to the right,' said the landlord. 'End of the path.'

Moments later I was back on the street and walking up a narrow lane to a row of cottages. I knocked on the door, then stood back to wait for someone to answer.

'Mrs Starr, is it?' I said, when a woman appeared. 'Sorry to disturb you so late.' Thin and with an air of abject defeat, she had the look of someone old before her time. 'I gave a lift to your . . . to Mary,' I said.

A flash of alarm in her eyes, then despair.

'Oh no,' I thought I heard her say.

From inside the small house, a man's rough voice, slurred with drink.

'Who is it?'

'Go away,' she whispered, trying to close the door. 'Leave us alone.'

'I'm sorry,' I said, a little nettled by her rudeness. 'I haven't explained myself properly. I picked up Mary on Harting Hill not five minutes ago. I'm sure it's a mistake, but when she got out of the car, she forgot to give my jacket back.'

'She's not here,' the woman said. 'How could she be?'

'I pulled up in the square,' I said, 'and she just hopped out. Five minutes ago, ten at most.'

Again, the drunk bellowing from the front room.

'Who the hell is it?'

'Go, please go,' she said, desperate this time. 'She's not here.'

I didn't want to cause trouble between this downtrodden woman and her husband.

'At least tell me if she's not here, where else might she be?'

For an instant, the haunted look in her eyes gave way to something else. Grief, perhaps. Resignation, maybe.

'The church,' she said softly.

This caught me out. 'So late?'

'Where else would she be?'

I heard the sound of a bolt being shot, then a heart-rending sob. I raised my hand to knock again, then let it drop. The woman was clearly terrorised by her brute of a husband. Perhaps Mary was too scared to go home?

*

I walked back to the High Street. The Ship Inn and the White Hart had called last orders and one or two rag-taggle farm workers were calling their goodnights into the damp night air.

One of the black wrought-iron gates into the churchyard was ajar, as if someone had recently slipped through. I pushed it open, thinking Mary might have taken refuge here after all. But the door stayed shut when I rattled the heavy cast-iron handle. I stepped out into the graveyard. Neat headstones closer to the church, rather more overgrown in the corners. Yew and mulberry and evergreen hedges. By an imposing flint wall, a row of older gravestones like broken teeth, a little crooked and sinking back into the earth.

I sensed movement. I narrowed my eyes and tried to adjust my vision to the darkness. Another fox? A sound in the under-growth, little more than that.

'Mary?'

I skirted the building and walked towards the sound. The bottom of my trousers grew damp with the dew from the grass and the cold night air slipped beneath my collar, but I paid no attention.

'Mary, is that you?'

I rounded the corner and found myself in a more secluded section of the graveyard. Stone angels and crosses, the flat tombs of an older age, and a few modern headstones. I could see no one, just shadows, phantasms in the intermittent moon-light.

No one.

But there was something moving, swaying in the breeze, something hanging on one of the gravestones. My jacket. I walked forward, then leant down to take it from the headstone.

Forced myself to read the inscription, though I feared what it was going to say.

MARY STARR
3rd OCTOBER 1931 – 27th OCTOBER 1951
IN GOD'S CARE

Bill tells me they found me there in the morning, clutching my jacket to my chest. I had a slight fever, a chill from spending the night out of doors. I wasn't ill, but not quite right either.

A local had seen my car still parked in the square, remembered me asking for directions to the Starr's house and put two and two together. It wasn't the first time, you see.

*

Bill came to fetch me – his number was on the map still lying on the passenger seat of the car. I stayed with him for a few days until I felt well enough to drive back to town. He told me the whole story. Mary had been seen before, always on the same stretch of road, always on the anniversary of her death. A local girl, Mary Starr, killed on Harting Hill ten years before. Hit and run in the days before there were such things. Or had she simply lost her footing and fallen? No one was sure. A sweet girl, innocent, who had gone for a drive with a local boy and without her father's permission. When the boy wouldn't take no for an answer and put her out of the car, Mary had no choice but to walk home in the worst storm they'd suffered for years. He raised the alarm when rumours spread that Mary had never arrived. Rain and mudslides, flooding on the lower roads, her body not found for days.

*

This happened some time ago. And although I was haunted by thoughts of Mary lost on the hillside, the memory of that night and my role in bringing her home is less troubling now.

Several years have passed. I married again, happily this time, and we have a wonderful daughter. Bright, charming, works hard at school. My wife says I am overprotective, and perhaps I am. From time to time, when we drive down to spend a weekend with Bill and his wife, he teases me about it too, though he understands.

I don't believe in ghosts, never did. All the same, each time I pass through South Harting, I stop at the church. To lay flowers on the grave of a girl I once met.

Author's Note

This story, written for the collection, was inspired by an experience I had more than thirty years ago.

I was driving home to Chichester, in Sussex. It was late at night, I hadn't long passed my driving test and as I went through the village of South Harting, The Specials were singing 'Ghost Town' on the radio.

When I turned to go up Harting Hill, a mist descended. I allowed myself to become completely spooked and started to worry what I'd do if the car broke down and I was stuck there on my own. This was 1981 and there were no mobile phones.

The car didn't break down. The mist lifted. Nothing happened. But I've never forgotten that journey and the illogical sense of threat in the darkness.

THE *PRINCESS ALICE*

Deptford, south-east London

September 1998

The *Princess Alice*

The bosun pipes the watch below,
Yeo ho! lads! ho!
Then here's a health afore we go
A long, long life to my sweet wife an' mates at sea;
And keep our bones from Davy Jones, where'er we be

from the ballad 'Nancy Lee' performed
aboard the *Princess Alice*, September 1878

The girl was crying again. A desolate sound of great grief, devoid of any hope, a child abandoned.

I sat up in bed, trying to identify where it was coming from. Somewhere nearby. I couldn't bear to hear it and do nothing.

I leant over and shook my husband's shoulder.

'There,' I whispered, 'she's here again. Can't you hear her? The same as before.'

He stirred. We listened. But now, though I could hear the traffic on the Broadway and two lads shouting about a taxi, I could no longer hear the weeping of a child.

'It's nothing,' he said. 'Someone in the street, that's all. Don't let it bother you.'

Rob rolled over and went back to sleep, leaving me sitting in the dark, knees drawn up, wondering if I was going bonkers. It was the third time in a week I'd been woken by the desperate sobbing. I glanced at the clock: five minutes past one in the morning, just like before.

This was our first flat and we loved it. A one-bedroom in a modern block conversion in Glaisher Street overlooking the Thames, good value for money, excellent transport links to the City for Rob's work and cycling distance to the University of Greenwich campus where I was due to take up a new teaching job in a couple of weeks' time. We'd only moved in at the end of August, but I'd met all of the neighbours already. Like us, they were mostly in their twenties and concentrating on their careers. None of them had children.

I leaned back against the wall. So why could I hear a little girl crying? Who was she?

*

Rob didn't mention it in the morning and neither did I.

We went through the usual morning rituals – shower and shaving, a shared pot of coffee, a peck on the cheek and a smell of aftershave.

'I'll be back by six,' he said. 'Seven tops. Fancy Chinese?'

I smiled. 'I thought we might go out. Find somewhere nice by the river. See what there is.'

'Sounds good,' he said. 'Let's play it by ear. I'll call.'

I nodded. 'OK,' I said. 'Have a good day.'

*

Since it wasn't raining, I went out for a walk. I wanted to get to know our new neighbourhood before the demands of time-tables, students, marking, colleagues took over. Once term started, I knew I'd have no time to explore. To get under the skin of the place.

I headed towards Lewisham first, following the Ravens-bourne, one of London's old forgotten rivers, then doubled back parallel to Brookmill Road. A smell of stale beer seeped out of the pub at the bottom of St John's Vale. In the morning sunshine, a cellar man clanked and rolled his empty barrels into the waiting lorry, a cigarette balanced on his lower lip. Along Cranbrook Road and over Friendly Street, through the white clapboard estate towards Tanner's Hill and Wellbeloved the Butcher, then on to Deptford Broadway.

Deptford Church Street was shut for the weekly market, so the traffic was heavy. All the lorries on their way to Dover, the salesmen in their clean company cars, jackets hanging from the hooks in the back, tapping their fingers impatiently on the steering wheel.

I held my breath, trying not to inhale the diesel and petrol fumes.

For a fraction of a second, nobody moved, then the lights turned green and the front runners surged out of the gates, up the hill towards Blackheath.

As the whine of the engines grew fainter, I found myself wondering if any of the drivers had even noticed the tiny streets through which they were driving. Did they see the stories beneath the cobbles and all the wharf buildings, the distinctive character of this corner of south-east London? Or did they only notice the booze shops hidden behind metal grilles, the burger joint and 24-hour supermarket where the drunks congregated, trying to make friends with anyone fool-ish enough to make eye contact.

*

A piece of urban art – what town planners and the *Daily Mail* call a 'feature' – sat at the top of Deptford Church Street. A large wrought-iron anchor set in stone, reminding shoppers of the district's maritime past. Two boys and a girl were clamber-ing all over it, hooking their legs over the arms, hanging upside down like monkeys. The hoods of their coats flopped over their faces and muffled their childish giggles.

And, with that, the memory of my broken sleep slipped back into my mind. The girl who cried in the night. I wondered who and where she was. Why no one did anything to comfort her. Rob thought I was making something out of nothing and I supposed he was right. Sound carries in the small hours, so the fact that there were no children in our block didn't mean anything. There were plenty of families living nearby. But as I walked back towards Glaisher Street, the oddness of it – the fact that I always heard her at the same time, the fact that Rob hadn't ever heard her – and nor had any of the neighbours – played on my mind.

The market was now in full swing. Men shouting into micro-phones, selling toasters, dinner sets and sofas. You want it, they'd got it. I negotiated my way between the two rows of stalls, their red and white plastic awnings rustling and flapping in the wind. There was even someone selling Jesus. Bibles, embroidered pic-tures with Christ's face stitched in bright gold thread on shiny black material, a pauper's Turin Shroud. CDs of gospel music proclaiming the happy day and a man, half preaching, half singing, welcoming in the lost souls. It seemed to be working – the stall was surrounded by women and their shopping trolleys. Just fifty pence per prayer or three for a pound: a bargain.

I ducked to avoid the halal meat hanging out over the pavement and tried not to catch the bulging eye of the red snapper and hake and salt fish in their white crates outside the fishmonger. I looked up, above the bustle of the market, and saw the curve of the Regency houses. The bricks were pale now, faded from their glory days when the docks were thriving and Deptford was a place with prospects. When I looked down, I saw blood leaking from the fish and meat into the gutter.

We hadn't completely unpacked – and I knew the last thing we needed was any more books – but I couldn't resist going, just to look, at the second-hand sellers who set up shop outside the Albany. There, the traders flogged their house clearances. A family's history for sale, wholesale, entire lives sold off to pay for the coffin.

Huge boarded tables took up most of one side of the square, every inch covered with junk. In the middle, a fifty-year-old woman with a suspicious face sat perched on an iron stool, watching the many hands fingering her wares, picking things up, putting things down, checking for damage or brand names. A Barbie with no hair, a pair of horseshoe bookends, brass hooks, pirate videos claiming to be ex-rental. Sold as seen, no guarantees.

Buyer beware.

The scavengers held things up and waited for Dee to catch their eye. She never engaged in conversation, just snapped the price. Quid, one-fifty, six for a quid. No negotiation. Like a ringmaster in a circus, she remained alert to the possibility that the animals circling could turn on her.

There were plenty of adults browsing the Albany plaza, accompanied by bored children who chased each other up and down between the stalls. A pale, thin girl in a long coat, down to the ground, and lace-up boots, was standing alone and ignored by the others.

I headed for one of the traders in the middle of the square. His quality books were displayed in rows on a table, but he'd tipped the rest onto an old red curtain spread on the ground.

'Ten for a pound, love,' he said when I got close.

I nodded, though I knew anyway. Last week, I'd picked up a faded leather-bound 1904 edition of *Bleak House* and a carrier bag full of Agatha Christies, Ngaio Marshes and Gladys Mitchells. I bent down and started to work systematically through the piles, focused and methodical as I moved books from place to place, careful not to hurry. If a book spiked my interest, I checked the pages weren't stuck together or missing, that bits of food or worse weren't pressed between its covers. If it got a clean bill of health, I put it with the 'definites' or the 'definite maybes'.

Perhaps there was a better selection than usual, but I went into what Rob called my 'book trance'. Book after book went on the pile. I was unaware of what was going on around me and of the weather turning. Didn't notice everyone else heading for cover. I didn't hear the rumbling in the sky or how the light drizzle had turned to rain, how the awnings pegged over the tables were being snagged and twitched by the wind.

'It's about to chuck it down any minute now, love. You done?'

I looked up with a start. 'I'm sorry, yes. I'll take these.'

I started to weed out the books I'd put aside.

'Call it ten. Need to cover this lot up.'

'That's kind of you.'
'That'll be a quid. Need a bag?'

*

Rather than getting soaked, I ducked into a table in a café by St Paul's Church to wait for the rain to pass.

The plate glass windows were already steamed up, the consequence of too many people in too little space. Outside clouds of umbrellas jostled, green and red and white and blue as people rushed for shelter. The traders had thrown black bin liners over their stock, hoping the storm would be done quickly and let them get back to earning a living.

I stood in the queue at the till, which got longer as more people splattered in, stamping their dripping feet on the mat and shaking umbrellas out the door. I noticed the same thin girl from the market, tracing her name on the window, and wondered why she didn't come in out of the wet. By the time I'd paid for my coffee and found a seat, she'd gone and the letters were smudged.

I hadn't paid attention to the last few books I'd bought, so I stuck my hand into the carrier bag and pulled out the one on the top. I didn't remember the look of it at all or picking it up, but it looked interesting. Not even a book, instead it was a diary. Or, rather, a record of events. Thin spidery writing, a few dates, all cramped up as if the writer didn't think she'd ever have enough paper to finish.

This is the private property of Miss Alice Sarah Livett,
Glaisher Street, Deptford, S.E.
If lost please return to rightful owner.

I smiled, intrigued by the coincidence of the address, then started to flick through the journal. The back pages were filled with columns, the weekly housekeeping accounts of everything required for the household in Glaisher Street, I assumed. Cloth, firewood, coal, horsemeat, wax, rum – I screwed up my eyes to decipher the tiny letters – and, next to each entry, the cost.

I flicked back to the beginning and found a list of birthdays and important events. Different colours of ink and subtle changes in the handwriting gave the impression that the list had been built up over many years.

15th May 1870. Robert William Livett to Isobel Grace Harris. Married St Paul's Church, Deptford.

18th June 1871. Alice Sarah. Born Glaisher Street.

20th June 1873. Nancy Grace. Born Glaisher Street.

24th May 1874. Hilda Eugenie. Born Glaisher Street.

17th February 1878. Florence Isobel. Born Glaisher Street.

3rd September 1878. Princess Alice.

19th September 1903. R. W. Livett to Mary Chalker. Married St Paul's Church, Deptford.

20th May 1904. Grace Charlotte. Born Evelyn Street.

The calendar filled several pages. It contained few references to anything outside Alice's immediate circle of family and neighbours and royalty. Day trips, visits to and from Glaisher Street, local events. The death of Queen Victoria was recorded, as was the Jubilee of King George V in 1935, but most national and world events went unremarked. Even the First and Second World Wars did not appear.

I glanced at the final entry.

25th November 1944. Woolworth's with G.

There was no explanation as to why Alice had suddenly stopped writing.

It was raining harder than ever so I looked to the counter, hoping the queue had died down so I could get another coffee. There were more people, though, so I kept reading and hoped no one would ask me to move.

By skimming backwards and forwards between the dates at the front and the diary entries themselves, I began to build up a picture of Alice's life. She was the eldest of four daughters – the other three didn't appear in the journal except at the beginning, and her mother was never mentioned, though her father was from time to time. At the age of fourteen, Alice was apprenticed to a local dressmaker, but continued living with her father in Glaisher Street and was still there when he remarried in 1903. There was no more than a handful of references to the second Mrs Livett, and the care of Grace, the child of that remarriage, in the Evelyn Street house, seemed to have fallen to Alice.

It was an odd experience reading about places I knew, or was starting to, and though things had changed hugely in a hundred years, I could still imagine Alice walking these same streets. I could picture the tramlines and the big shops in Lewisham and New Cross, could imagine the gentle, confined pace of Alice's life lived in and around Deptford. From the journal, it seemed neither Alice nor her younger half-sister Grace ever married, but both were regular church goers and members of various Bible groups who met in the Wesleyan Hall round the back of Sayes Court. Day trips with local schoolchildren to the seaside in 1925. Not Margate or Southend, but upriver to the mudflats by Tower Bridge to make mud-and-sand pies in the sunshine.

The second Mrs Livett died in 1925 and, after a long illness, Alice's father followed her a year later. And there, in Alice's diary entry for the day before his death, was the record of a conversation between father and daughter. The only personal entry of any kind.

It sent me back to the beginning and the list of dates.

3rd September 1878. Princess Alice.

The entry had stuck out the first time I'd read it because it didn't seem to belong in the list of family birthdays and anniversaries. Now, though, from Alice's record of the penultimate day of her father's life, it was clear the date mattered a great deal.

Without considering the luck that had brought such a journal into my hands in the first place, never mind the coincidence of our living in the same street as the author of the diary, I packed up.

*

Ten minutes later I was home and sitting in front of the computer.

Beyond the window, the Thames was still shrouded in low cloud and smears of drizzle ran down the window. I typed in the date and waited for information to come up, watched the images and words roll onto the screen.

On Tuesday, 3rd September, 1878, the London Steamboat Company's pleasure paddle steamer, the *Princess Alice*, sailed on a day trip to Gravesend and Sheerness. Among the seven hundred passengers were a Mrs Hawks, the owner of the Anchor and Hope pub at Charlton, a group of 'ladies of the night' from the Seven Dials area of London, forty women from Smithfield's Crowcross Mission and a group from a Bible class which included Mrs Isobel Livett and three of her daughters, Florence, Nancy and Hilda, aged seven months, five and four respectively. The eldest daughter, Alice, had stayed home to look after Mr Livett, who was not well enough to join the party.

My chest tightened. I dreaded reading on, yet I couldn't stop.

At seven-thirty in the evening, the steamer was approaching Gallion's Reach. Many of the passengers, in good spirits from their day out, were below deck in the restaurant bar listening to the live entertainment. Accompanied by a ramshackle choir made up of the steamer's crew, a tenor was performing Maybrick's ballad 'Nancy Lee'.

As the steamer rounded the bend between Crossness and Margaret Ness near Tripcock Point, she met the steam collier, *Bywell Castle*. The collier had just off-loaded her cargo at Millwall Dock and was returning to the South Shore.

The *Princess Alice* was new in 1865. It was originally licensed to carry 486 passengers, increased after a refit in 1878 to 936. The Board of Trade considered one lifeboat and one longboat to provide adequate safety precautions, despite the fact they could carry no more than sixty people apiece. The collier ploughed full steam into the *Princess Alice*, splitting her down the middle. There was no time to sound the alarm and no time to alter course. The stern and bows folded upwards and, within minutes, the pleasure steamer had sunk, taking almost everyone with her.

Children and women, mostly unable to swim, were pulled

down by their crinolines and skirts and few made it to the shore, even though it was only three hundred yards away. Others survived, only to be swept downstream in the ebb tide to drown in the polluted waters from the Southern Outfall works near Erith.

The bodies brought ashore were taken mainly to Woolwich Dockyard and Roff's Wharf and given numbers until they could be identified. Some corpses drifted as far as Gravesend, where they were laid for claiming in the pier waiting room. Later, a large Celtic cross was raised at Woolwich Cemetery by public subscription, 23,000 people giving sixpence each to make a grave for the 160 unclaimed victims. Others were buried by their families at St John's Church in Lewisham and St Paul's Church in Deptford, including four members of a well-regarded family living in Glaisher Street. The newspaper noted that when the police arrived to inform Mr Livett of the tragic accident at five past one, on the morning of the following day, he suffered a seizure and was unable to leave the house. In the absence of any other adult, his only surviving daughter – seven-year-old Alice Livett – was obliged to identify the bodies of her mother and her sisters.

I turned cold. Five minutes past one in the morning.

My mind racing, I sat back in my chair, trying to piece everything together: the timing of the police's arrival, the collapse of Mr Livett at the news, the fact that Deptford had been badly damaged during bombing in World War II. Most of the houses on the river had been flattened. Was it possible that our block stood where once Alice Livett had lived? Could it be her cries I heard at night? Or rather, the echo of her grief? And if so, why? Because she had been forgotten? Because the story had been forgotten?

I glanced out of the window and saw the rain had stopped. I put my coat back on and left the flat. With Alice's journal in my hand, I headed back to St Paul's.

The sun had come out now, causing the wet grass to glint and giving the impression of everything having been washed clean and made new. There was no guide to the graves in the churchyard and the church itself was locked, so I could find no one to ask about parish registers. I walked up and down, reading each name on the headstones, tracing the faded dates with my fingers, looking for Alice and her family.

Finally, I found what I was looking for. Three headstones in a row, close to the back wall of the churchyard. The first commemorated Isobel Livett and her daughters Nancy, Hilda and Florence, who had died in the wreck of the *Princess Alice* on 3rd September 1878; the second was for Robert Livett and his second wife, Mary, who had died a year before him in 1925. And the third . . .

Tears pricked my eyes.

The inscription on the stone explained why the journal had suddenly stopped. The third grave remembered Alice Livett and her half-sister Grace, both of whom had lost their lives in the V2 bombing of the Woolworth's Department Store on New Cross Road on 25th November 1944.

Tragedy had struck this one family twice. Alice, her mother, and all four of her sisters had been killed. No wonder Glaisher Street held the imprint of such sorrow.

I took a pencil from my pocket and added the dates of the day Alice and Grace had died to the front of the journal. It made no difference to the ending, of course, but it finished the story. Their deaths recorded properly, as they should be.

I closed the pages and looked around at the peaceful church, caught between the hum of traffic on Creek Road and the Broadway. I thought of all the lives lived in the tiny streets which lay beneath the modern roads. I thought I might donate the journal to a local history association who'd be glad to have it. And how the everyday lives of women and men mattered every bit as much as those of kings and queens and politicians. Should not be overlooked.

I was now certain that Alice's house once stood where I had now made my home. That it was her I heard crying at night. How she wanted not to be forgotten.

And as I walked slowly home, I cast my eyes around, hoping again to see a glimpse of the thin, pale girl who had been at the market, perhaps who had even put her diary into my bag. Who had watched me in the café, seen me open the journal.

She wasn't there.

*

Later, Rob and I found a restaurant on the water and watched the sun go down. He talked about his day and asked if I'd heard from the university. We shared a bottle of white wine.

At ten o'clock, we settled the bill and walked down Glaisher Street towards home.

'If it's really bothering you,' he said a little awkwardly, 'you know, the noise, I'll speak to the caretaker. I'm sure there's something he can do. No sense having sleepless nights.'

I threaded my arm through his and squeezed. 'It's all right,' I said. 'I have a feeling it won't be a problem any more.'

I didn't think she would come again. Now I knew who she was and why she was stricken with such grief, she had no need.

'You've found out where the sound's coming from?'

'Not exactly.'

Rob frowned. 'But you know who she is?'

'Yes,' I smiled. 'A girl who needs to be remembered, just like all of us. A girl called Alice.'

Author's Note

Although this is a new story, it's based on notes I made back in 1998. At that stage, I'd published two non-fiction books and two novels, both of them well enough received, but I hadn't yet found my voice as a writer of fiction. Coming upon these scribbled notes fifteen years later, it's interesting to see how I was starting to experiment with a style of writing that I was to develop in my Languedoc Trilogy and *The Winter Ghosts*: namely, the use of real history to inspire an imaginary story, the device of a timeslip – characters separated by more than a hundred years, but connected through living in the same place; the notion that stories come out of landscape (or, in this case, the cityscape); the hope that emotion will speak across boundaries of time and context, one generation to the next, the sense that the human heart does not change so very much.

Behind the notes was a conviction that history should be the story of us all, not simply a recitation of kings and queens and generals. Even the most significant events will, if not written down, fade from common memory. We were living in Deptford, in the south-east of London, when I came across the real history of the wreck of the pleasure steamer the *Princess Alice*. A huge catastrophe in 1878, and much covered by the contemporary newspapers, it is one of those pieces of local history that has since faded from public knowledge.

IN THE THEATRE AT NIGHT

Shaftesbury Avenue, London
November 1930

In the Theatre at Night

Things have their own lives here.

from 'Dispossessions'
JANE COOPER

Soft the night and the watchman carries his lamp through the sleeping theatre.

The audience has gone home, in stoles and dress coats and gloves. Carriages and footfall along the Strand and Shaftesbury Avenue, heading to Hyde Park and Soho and Kensington. The velvet red is returned to its pristine condition in the stalls and the dress circle and the benches up in the gods. The footlights are dark, no flare of sulphur or blue spurts of gas. Glass and gilt, cerulean blues and peacock purples, the painted landscape of the safety curtain, all dull and flat without the lights to bring their colours to life.

An empty theatre is a space stripped of purpose. It holds within its hushed air the echo of all the feet that have trodden the space between the rows, the spirits linger. Memory of programmes trimmed with gold ribbon and opera glasses released for a penny, feathers and silver-topped canes, the champagne corks in the boxes and the sweet wrappers in the one and nines. The hush of the pass door between the real world and the glittering artifice beyond. The smell of wood and greasepaint, the brushes and hangers and spirit gum in the wings, the plaster of Paris feasts of duck and fruit that has no taste, the metallic tang of swords awaiting hands to give them purpose.

The minutes pass, midnight tipping into one o'clock. Twenty past one, a quarter to two. The old watchman sits at the stage door, a muffler round his neck and his hands close to the heater, a nip of whisky, and tongue sandwiches made by his wife to get him through the small hours. The bell in the tower of St Anne's chimes the hour over the streets of Soho. Two o'clock and all's well.

A paperback novel is open on his lap. Henri Bencolin keeps him company. A locked room in a Paris gambling house, a mangled body on the floor, a severed head staring from the centre of the carpet, it's a good puzzle. He reads, turning the pages with cold fingers, and the time between one circuit of the theatre and the next, the time stretches wider.

In the dead of night, there's not a soul about. All the doors are locked and the customers have gone home. The actors are tucked up in bed or drinking with the girls from the Palace Theatre round the corner or with the poets and the playwrights in the Wardour Street gambling houses.

His head starts to droop. The book slips from his fingers to his lap, then onto the floor.

*

This is when it happens. When there's no longer anyone watching or clapping or breaking the spell, the theatre comes to life.

In Wardrobe, the costumes begin to move. The kirtle and the peplos, the chiton and the farthingale. The colours of the past – madder for red, woad for blue or walnut for brown. Crinolines and corsets, feathers. First French empire, boots and neckties, plus fours and Fair Isles, all the ages of woman and of man, held on wooden hangers ready for the next time they are required.

They carry within them the imprint of every actor, each actress, who has pushed their arms into the sleeves, who has been stitched or pressed or ironed or sculpted into the cloth. No human ear can hear the music, but now they are moving, the costumes of every production that has graced these boards, coming back to waltz and to polka and to molly dance across the stage. They know each other well. For season after season, they have found themselves dyed and taken in and let out, cut and refitted to suit the players who are passing through.

They outlive us all, the wool and the silk and the cotton. Within their seams, they know how Desdemona died or Brutus betrayed, they know the outline of Mrs Malaprop as well as they know an Elyot Chase. They do not stay in one place, any more than do the actors.

Now the stage is alive again. With dancing, with movement, with speech and thought. The shadows, the ghosts, of all the women and men who have stepped into the spotlight and spoken words of love and of regret, of hate and humour, every sentiment and sentence remembered is now played out again upon these boards.

Around and around they coil and weave and twine, re-membering their friendships and love affairs, gentle about the people who have inhabited the costume, knowing that each one has left an imprint. The band plays on, one minute brassy and coarse, the next falling into gentle and sinuous melodies. Major to minor, the beat changing with each tap of the conductor's baton on the stand.

*

It is six in the morning and the watchman is stirring. He jerks awake, stretches, sees the novel on the floor and realises he dozed off as usual.

On the stage, the costumes sigh and look at one another. Like children to bed, they regretfully take their leave. A bow, a cuff unfurled, a skirt curtsied, a gentle withdrawal. The cue has been given. The light of another day is seeping through the gaps in the window frames, beneath the door frame and the skylight.

Soon, it will be morning. Soon, the coopers and the milk boys and the barrow boys will be out, wheels over the cobbled stones, the pale yellow sunlight rising over London.

The watchman staggers to his feet and stretches, prepares to do his rounds. As he wanders through the empty passageways of the theatre, he thinks things don't look quite as he left them. He chalks that down to his memory. It does not occur to him that the objects we surround ourselves with have lives of their own.

Author's Note

I've always felt that one of the most exciting places in the world is backstage in a theatre.

At school and university, I spent a great deal of time backstage – being 'helpful'. Moving props, negotiating for the hire of scaffolding or clothes, wine or printing of programmes. I had no talent as a performer, but that sense in theatre that every night something unique, something special, might happen – and wanting to be part of it – has never left me.

Thirty years later, a fledgling playwright now, I am still beguiled by the idea that the fixtures and fittings of a theatre – the costumes and wigs, the props and the armoury – might know more than the people who come to direct and produce, act and usher. The sense of a secret life, the belief that the fabric and architecture of a place is more important than the transience of people who come and go, is very attractive.

This is both the shortest of the stories in the collection and the most gentle. It is deliberately old-fashioned, inspired by a belief that possessions carry an imprint of all those who have come into contact. What Neil MacGregor calls 'the charisma of things'*, it's the beguiling idea that we could pick up a brooch or a sword, put on a coat or pick up a bus ticket and be connected to someone decades, centuries, ago.

* Neil MacGregor, *Shakespeare's Restless World* (Penguin, 2012)

THE YELLOW SCARF

Minster Lovell Hall, Oxfordshire
October 1975

The Yellow Scarf

A serious house on serious earth it is,
In whose blent air all our compulsions meet,
Are recognised, and robed as destinies

from 'Church Going'
PHILIP LARKIN

Once she was sure nothing was going on, Sophia pushed open the door and went inside. A pleasing smell of must and antiquity – parchment and stone, candles with the wicks burnt low. The air infused with the scent of incense long gone.

The chapel was empty. She slipped into the pew closest to the door, feeling the hard press of the wood through her thin summer coat, and exhaled. Five minutes to herself.

Sophia was accompanying her aunt on a coach tour of minor stately homes. A week's holiday from work, all expenses paid. For the most part, she was enjoying herself. A small independent company, designed for 'the more mature' traveller, they were visiting the less well-known, less celebrated houses – none of the Blenheims or Chatsworths or Burghleys. The brochure promised four counties in seven days: Hampshire,

Berkshire, Wiltshire and Oxfordshire, the so-called 'Cradle of England'. Sophia's aunt was sharp as a pin and self-sufficient – and the other retired ladies and two gentlemen in the party were lovely – but Sophia was finding it a little tiring to be always in company. Also, since most of her aunt's friends were a little hard of hearing, the constant leaning forward in her seat and shouting over the thrumming of the engine as the coach made its way through Oxfordshire, had given Sophia a headache. Since most of the party had opted to take a look at the famous Charterville Allotments in the village of Minster Lovell, it was a chance to have some time to herself. There were two more visits scheduled for the afternoon – then an illustrated talk *with slides* (this picked out in italics in the itinerary) over dinner in Oxford that night – it was likely to be her only chance today for a little peace and quiet.

She'd been particularly looking forward to this visit to the ruins of a medieval manor house on the outskirts of the village. There was rumoured to be some distant family link with the place. Like all such stories, it came from the coincidence of their shared surname, rather than anything based in history or fact, but Sophia liked the idea of a connection all the same.

She placed her hands in her lap, shut her eyes and let the timeless calm wash over her. She took deep breaths, feeling her shoulders rise and fall, clearing her mind of schedules and tea shops and 'comfort breaks'. Gradually, the band of pain behind her eyes loosened its grip. Sophia could hear the song of the River Windrush outside, chasing over stone and branch and bank. And in her mind's eye, too, half-caught sounds echoing back through the centuries.

There wasn't much in her guidebook about Minster Lovell

Hall. Owned by the Lovell family in the thirteenth and fourteenth centuries, the estate had changed hands after the Battle of Bosworth in 1485. The House of Lancaster defeating the House of York, the fall of the Plantagenet dynasty and the ascendancy of the Tudors, the Lovell family had refused to put their faith in Henry, then Duke of Richmond. Their lands were forfeit to the Crown, passing into the hands of the Coke family, then fallen into disrepair centuries later.

Sophia didn't remember mention of a separate family chapel – since St Kenelm's Church and graveyard were so close, she couldn't see there would have been much need for a place of worship set away from the house. But as she sat now, in the small chapel, she found it easy to imagine flickering candles and a servant going ahead to light the way in the dark to this tiny stone building.

More intriguing was the folklore that a young bride – married to a nobleman called Lovell – was said to have disappeared here on her wedding night. In one version of the story, she had simply vanished during the feast and never been seen again. In another, a skeleton still dressed in bridal clothes was discovered in a hidden space between the walls of the ruined house by workmen in the eighteenth century: a murder or accident, no one knew. A fragment of history, or legend? No one seemed to know. Even so, in the peaceful silence of the chapel, it piqued Sophia's interest in her surroundings.

Five minutes turned to ten. Feeling a pleasant drowsiness, a prickling at the base of her neck, and knowing she couldn't allow herself to drop off, Sophia reluctantly opened her eyes. She only had an hour and a half before the coach came back to pick them up and she wanted to explore the grounds and ruins themselves too.

She looked at her watch. Tapped the glass with her finger-nail. The minute hand had been sticking for days, but usually she could jolt it back into life. She tapped again, but this time nothing happened. It had stopped. It was a nuisance – their days were organised to the minute – but Sophia didn't think she'd been in the chapel very long. Promising herself to find a jeweller's in Oxford later to replace the battery, Sophia undid the strap, put the watch in her coat pocket and then stood to have a quick look around the chapel.

There was nothing of particular merit. Four plaques with the coat of arms of the Lovell family, a hound in flight, and a wooden bas-relief in the chancel – Sophia picked out a swan and a dove, an animal that might have been a hart or a stag, and a female figure in long, ornate robes. Sophia peered closely. Here was evidence linking the story of the vanished bride to Minster Lovell Hall. Long ribbons threaded through her hair, a beaded dress, slippers on her feet. In her hands, a wedding wreath of winter holly and mistletoe.

Sophia held the young bride's gaze for a little longer, then moved on. Two brass candlesticks stood on the modest altar with a wooden lectern standing beside. A standard King James Bible, which suggested the chapel was still in use long after the Lovell family had renounced their claims to the estate.

Sophia gave a final glance, then turned and retraced her steps. At the door she paused, noticing an inscription carved on the wooden frame.

Our brief partings on earth will appear one day as nothing beside the joy of eternity together

Then she noticed a few words had been added underneath in black paint, almost rubbed away in places:

Lost but not forgotten

A piece of historic graffiti, if the ragged and inconsistent size of the letters were anything to go by. Sophia smiled, carried back to a summer long ago. Herself at seven years old – smocked dress, white ankle socks, the feel of cold metal in her hand – carving her name and the date on the bark of a tree with her brother's penknife: SOPHIA P LOVELL 1955. Her mother had smacked her, yet it had seemed worth it. That all too human desire to stand out, to stamp one's mark on a place. The fifteenth century, the twentieth, some things never changed. That fierce need in all of us to be remembered.

She peered closer, hoping for a date or name, but there was nothing to reveal who had added the words or for whom.

*

The sky had clouded over while she'd been inside and there was now an unseasonable chill in the air. Everything looked dull and grey. Sophia shivered. As she walked back through the avenue of trees, the world seemed bleached of colour. No sun burnishing the leaves of the beeches that stood at the furthest edges of the lawns, no birdsong. And the path between them seemed longer than before, the twisting branches that had provided a green canopy now oddly bare.

Sophia stopped. She wasn't sure how it could have happened, but she had somehow lost her bearings. She wasn't quite sure where she was. She thought back. The coach had left them on Manor Road, leaving Sophia and her three companions to make their own way past St Kenelm's church to the ruins of Minster Lovell Hall. She'd excused herself and struck out on her own, following a path through the graveyard towards the river before noticing the chapel and going there instead. Since there was only one door and the path led directly to it, there was no choice but to go in and come out the same way. It was nigh on impossible to have got lost. And yet Sophia had the distinct impression of being in a different place. Or, rather, the same place which no longer looked quite the same.

She looked at her wrist, forgetting her watch was broken and in her pocket, wondering if it was possible the others had left the grounds and taken a short cut through the graveyard of St Kenelm's. Rubbed the bare skin on her arm. Not that it mattered, she supposed, provided she was waiting at the right place for the coach at the appointed time. She didn't think it could be anywhere close to twelve yet and, besides, she'd hear the church bells chime.

With the river at her back, she orientated towards the north, fixing the jagged outline and pointed stone gables of Minster Lovell Hall clearly in her sights. With a pinch of relief, Sophia walked towards the ruins. The less tended lawns closer to the river bank gave way to geometric ornamental gardens and the remains of neat foundation walls of Cotswold stone. The variegated shades of autumn, burgundy and gold, had given way to bare trunks and a few defiant firs. Sophia looked again for sight of her companions, keen to be back in company again, but there was no sign of them.

With a shrug, she determined to make the most of the time she had left. Told herself not to let her imagination run away with her. According to her guidebook, the house itself had

taken shape over generations around three sides of a court-
yard, with a high blind wall on the river side. When she
reached the remains of a wide, circular well, and looked down
into the narrow space, it crossed her mind that it was all less
dilapidated than she'd expected. And as Sophia moved further into the body of the house, she found her sense of it
growing stronger.

She walked through a stone arch set into a wall and
along a vaulted corridor to the main hall. The roof was gone,
so the high arched windows seemed to hang adrift, like flags,
at the very top of the walls. Stone turned green by age and
ivy, the beauty of the fifteenth-century outline silhouetted
against the October sky. The remains of stairs leading up to
the family's private rooms.

Sophia turned and stepped back over one of the foundation
walls, but stumbled and nearly lost her balance. She glanced
down, then frowned. She could have sworn the outline of the
wall had been little more than a mark on the ground. Now, it
was several bricks high.

She shivered. It wasn't like her to be clumsy or out-of-sorts.
Her thin summer coat no longer seemed adequate. She tightened the belt and tucked her shiny yellow square scarf under
her collar to keep warmer, but she still felt cold. She put her
hand to her forehead, wondering if she was coming down with
something, but she didn't have a temperature. She didn't feel
ill, just chilly and rather odd. As if she was somehow watching
everything from behind a sheet of glass. Both part of things
and separate from them.

Increasingly uneasy, Sophia carried on. She refused to
allow nerves to get the better of her. Resolutely, she followed
a cobbled pathway which led to the north wing and through

a sequence of smaller rooms, with the hint of a small fireplace set into the north wall. On to the east wing, now breathing the scents of the stables and working places of the house. Leather and straw and guttering set into the ground, the scratch of the hot iron and the hiss of metal in the stone water tanks.

As Sophia walked, the colours and shadows seemed to deepen and take a more profound shape. The elegant ruined outlines of Minster Lovell Hall were coming back to life, or so it seemed: the leaping flames in the great stone fireplaces in the hall, the walls soaring high above, the beauty of the arched windows. The tapestries and wall hangings, long tables with candles and dishes laid for a banquet, sweet melody trickling down from the minstrels' dais. She could almost hear the song of lute and viol, citole and recorder, the mournful single beat of a drum.

Everywhere, white hawthorn and boughs of mistletoe.

Was this where the wedding feast had been held those hundreds of years before? Where a young bride had danced and been admired but then vanished? Sophia found herself looking into the empty space, imagining the ghostly outlines of men and of women, of servants and musicians, the lord of the manor and his retainers.

The mistletoe hung in the castle hall.

Shadow dancers, their features taking shape. Almost visible, almost returned. Sophia slowly moved on, feeling the unseen presence of others all around her, a prickling at the nape of her neck.

At last, she found herself at the foot of the tower that stood at the far south-west corner of the property. And she realised that her view of the gardens was obscured now by brick and stone.

The whispering was growing stronger, clearer.

A toast to the goodly company.

Sophia spun round and looked behind her. Still she could see no one, though she felt their presence strongly. Another flutter of nerves in her stomach: anticipation or premonition?

Now the echo of ancient words was clearer still, layered over the bristling disquiet of the day. Sounds of laughter and celebration, whispering and billowing and creaking of the old house. Footsteps on the flagstone floor, servants carrying and fetching, kitchen to table with dish after dish, doors opening and closing. A celebration, a feast.

Sophia felt the muscles in her stomach tighten. It wasn't merely that the house was shifting and changing its shape around her, but also that there was a growing tension in the air. Beneath the echo of sounds of celebration and good cheer was a sense of threat. The harmless process of imagining the house as it once was had become something else. A crack in time, a slipping between this world and another.

She looked at the stairs. She didn't want to go up, yet at the same time she felt she had no choice. Sophia took a deep breath, then put her hand against the rough stonework to anchor herself, and began to climb. Higher and higher she went, up into an octagonal turret nestled between the tower and the west wing. A mournful wind was crying in the gables and there was a bite in the air warning of snow. And when she looked out through the stone mullions of the window, there was a dusting of frost on the ground.

Sophia walked along a long corridor, towards the solar. Watching herself, as if from the outside, a woman in a cream coat and brown shoes, a yellow scarf knotted at her neck, heading towards a closed door.

Still the voices from the past called out to her. And again, the words of the old fireside song Sophia hardly remembered knowing.

The mistletoe hung in the castle hall.

*

Suddenly, without warning, the clanging of a bell cut through the domestic sounds of the house. Sophia stopped dead, the coarse alarum reverberating through her bones. Unseen hands pulling the bell rope in St Kenelm's Church, warning of danger. Warning that the village was under attack.

Sophia began to run towards the closed door.

From below, shouts broke out. She heard furniture being dragged across the stone entrance hall and bolts being fastened, orders to secure all entrances. The ghostly inhabitants of the house were defending Minster Lovell Hall as once they had five hundred years ago.

Now, a violent hammering at the front entrance, clenched fists, and a harsh voice demanding admittance.

In the name of the king.

The sound of wooden sticks beating on the door as the soldiers tried to force their way in.

Open up, by order of the king. In the name of the king.

Then, without touching anything or feeling anything, Sophia found herself on the far side of the door and standing in a small and modest space, a private rather than a public place. Here, was silence. And here, at last, she could see the outline of a person. A young woman, sitting on a plain wooden chair in the centre of the tiny room.

Sophia watched as the woman became clearer, her features growing definite and distinct, like a photograph developing in a darkroom. A fold of embroidery lay on a table close by, weft and warp, cotton threads of yellow and silver in the light of a single candle. Her hands were still. Her blond hair was braided and shot through with white ribbon and she wore a white kirtle, decorated with mother-of-pearl beads, the long skirts pooled around her feet.

Despite her thudding heart, Sophia realised she was smiling. For although the carving in the chapel had been crude, this woman was clearly the model for the image carved on the bas-relief. A winter wedding, all white and gold, the hall decked in hawthorn and mistletoe.

Sophia wanted to ask why she was sitting here alone and she tried to speak. Immediately she saw the young bride could no more hear her than she could see her and, in any case, she thought she understood. She was seeking a moment of solitude, just as Sophia had craved a morning free from the chitterings of her aunt's friends.

Wanting to forge some connection between her and the girl from the past, Sophia reached out. She encountered no resistance, just empty space, though as her hand fell back to her side, she felt the slightest of movements of cold air.

A sudden roar from down below. The sounds of assault and devastation finally reached their sanctuary. The stolen calm of the room was shattered. Once again, Sophia tried to speak, more urgent this time, but though the words formed in her throat, no sound came out.

Helpless, she looked at the girl, desperate for her to act. Her eyes were dark, with fear certainly, though not surprise. Sophia realised she had expected such an attack. Maybe not this day in particular, not her wedding night, but some time. She had known the soldiers would come.

Was that why she sat here alone? Had she been sent to the safety of the solar in case of such an attack?

Open up in the name of the king.

The tramp of men's boots thundering up the stairs. Within moments, they would find the room. Find the woman here alone.

Hide yourself, hide.

She willed the girl to hear her and, this time, though Sophia's words remained unspoken, she was on her feet. Quickly, she put her things away, wanting to leave no evidence the room had been so recently occupied. As she gathered her threads and sampler and stowed it inside a chest, a brass thimble fell from her fingers and rolled away into the furthest corner of the room. Sophia tried to retrieve it, wanting to help, but her fingers found only air.

Hurry, quick. Hide.

Leaving the thimble to the room, the girl blew out the candle and rushed to the heavy tapestry covering the largest of the walls. With a final glance at the bolted door, the bride lifted the corner and stepped behind. Sophia heard the spring of a catch and saw, in the moments before the girl disappeared into the dark, the secret compartment built within the space between the thick walls of the house.

The girl caught her breath, steeling herself for what she had to do, then she vanished from Sophia's sight. The snap of the door shutting, and it was as if she had never been.

Sophia felt a wave of relief. There was yet a chance the soldiers would not find her. Then, hard on its heels, a wash of cold dread as she remembered the legend in her guidebook. The story of a body entombed in the walls. A skeleton in bridal robes.

Sophia started towards the tapestry, but then heard the sound of the soldiers right outside the door. There was no choice but for the girl to remain hidden.

For now, only for now.

Sophia noticed the tapestry was crooked. Instinctively, she put out her hand to straighten it. Again, her fingers found only air.

Open up.

The latch rattled, the door straining against the bolt as the soldiers set their shoulders to the jamb. And although Sophia knew they couldn't see her, her palms were slippery with fear. She tried again and, this time, it seemed as if the tapestry moved a little. Moved enough.

In the name of the king.

The wooden frame around the door was starting to give. This domestic room within a private house was not built to withstand such treatment. Even though she knew it would make no difference, Sophia threw the full weight of her body against the door. She could not stand by and do nothing.

One final blow and the frame buckled, the door splintered from its hinge and the men burst through. Three soldiers with swords drawn and a fourth holding a flaming torch in his hand.

They snapped and snarled, like hunting dogs after prey, cheated to find the room empty.

Though she could barely breathe from fear, Sophia stood her ground. Whatever had happened five hundred years ago – if she was seeing an echo of things that had been – she was determined it would be different this time. Whatever tragedy had taken place in this room, she would not let the story have the same ending.

But she could only watch with mounting fear, mounting rage, as the soldiers ransacked the room, to teach the traitor Lovell a lesson. Upturning the table, breaking the lock on the chest and tramping the delicate red and blue and white threads under heel. Dashing the candlestick and earthenware goblet from the table until everything was broken and spoiled.

They stopped.

Sophia felt a flicker of hope. Perhaps, now, they would leave? Move on to the next room? Three of the soldiers did turn to withdraw, calling for their companion to follow them. He started after them, still holding the flame to light the way, then he stopped. His expression changed as he turned slowly back to the room.

For a moment, Sophia thought he somehow could see her. His eyes seemed to be cutting right through her. But then, to her horror, he began to walk towards the tapestry itself.

She tried to block his path. But her imprint was too faint and he kept on coming. Now he was reaching up and with rough hands, nails black with dirt, he ripped the tapestry from the wall with a single, jagged movement.

Sophia caught her breath. There was nothing visible. If she hadn't seen the girl disappearing into the hidden space with her own eyes, she wouldn't have known it was there. Washed with lime and uneven in the way of old houses, the wall looked unbroken. A pattern of thin lines and crosses covered the entire surface, like a spider's web, disguising the outline of the door perfectly.

The soldier held the flame closer, puzzled by the strange markings concealed beneath the tapestry. Sophia stepped between him and the wall, a barrier between him and the hidden girl. And though she still didn't think he could see her, she knew he sensed her presence. The peculiar sensation of the half touch of his fingers paddling across the surface of her skin.

He felt something too.

The soldier withdrew his hand, as if he'd been stung, and turned it over, examining his palm. Sophia had no idea what kind of superstitions or fears stalked his dreams at night, but the belligerence that had driven him into the room deserted him.

She breathed out, unable to stay completely still for an instant longer. The soldier reacted. He put his hand to his face, as if brushing a cobweb away.

Had he felt her breath on his skin?

She took a deep breath and, this time, blew directly into his face. He took a step back. Quickly, Sophia pulled the scarf from her neck and, as she blew out again, she also stirred the air with the yellow handkerchief.

This time, he cried out, flapping his hand at the empty air to ward off the evil spirits. Sophia waved the scarf from side to side, forcing him to jab the flame into the black. The soldier crossed himself, turned on his heel and fled.

The room was plunged back into darkness.

For an instant, Sophia didn't move. Her blood pounding in her ears, listening to the drum of his running feet until she could hear him no longer. Silence rushed back into the room.

Only then did her legs turn to water. Dizzy with relief, Sophia slumped back against the wall, heart hammering in her chest. She had done it. She had driven him away.

But her task was not yet finished.

Quickly, she turned and examined the wall, trying not to think about what the absence of sound from below might mean. The darkness surged around her, like a living, breathing

thing. Though her fingers skimmed the surface, she couldn't seem to touch, and she couldn't find any kind of switch or catch to release the door. With the increasing sense of urgency, she crouched down and tried to force her fingers into the gap between the bottom of the wall and the floorboards. Again, though she could feel her nerve endings and her muscles and her skin, her hands seemed to go straight through into thin air.

There had to be something she could do. She had driven the soldier away, even though the physical realities of blood and bone and muscle had no meaning here. Could not translate from one time to this other. But spirit?

Here was a place of spirit, the communion of souls. It was that the soldier had sensed, had felt.

Sophia slowly and deliberately took a deep breath, then exhaled. Nothing. She closed her eyes and, taking as much oxygen into her lungs as possible, she breathed out once more.

Again, nothing. She tried once more and, gradually, as she breathed in and out again, the room started to tilt and to shift and to pulse, until, suddenly, like a rush of wind in the trees, it was filled with movement.

Sophia opened her eyes.

The sensation of sound and shade and limitless space and as the roaring in the room grew louder, the candlestick was sent rolling across the floor, the goblet clattered into the wainscot. And now every piece of broken wood and trampled thread seemed part of the symphony. A drumming, notes between music, percussion and melody, calling whoever might be left to hear to this one corner of the west wing of the house.

Sophia kept breathing life into the room, out and in and out, like the song of the tide upon the shore, until at last she heard voices. From the corridor, a pool of light, getting stronger, and an old woman's voice calling out a name.

Perdita. My lady, Perdita.

Sophia turned cold, remembering the inscription written above the door in the chapel: lost but not forgotten.

Now the woman, bent low and in the plain clothes of a servant, was standing on the threshold, a candle held in a trembling hand.

Instantly, the room was still. The air fell silent.

She's here, quick.

The woman cried out at the sight of the coloured threads tangled and twisted on the floor, at the broken furniture, and the flame shook. Sophia called out again, even though she could not be heard, willing the old woman to turn and find the door and release the catch. But she didn't move. She merely stood in the middle of the room, her old eyes clouded with confusion.

My lady, Perdita.

Sophia knew her part in the story was nearly at an end. The outline of the room was fainter than before, less distinct. Minster Lovell Hall was returning to its current state, leaving the past behind. Condemning the bride to her living tomb.

She's here, here.

Then Sophia watched the expression on the old woman's face change. Willing her to turn, to keep looking, to not give up. The woman shuffled across the room and bent down to pick something up.

Her yellow scarf, lying precisely where Sophia knew the hidden door to be. She didn't understand how the woman could see it. It was caught on something, a nail or a splinter. She pulled again and, this time, the yellow square of material came free. At the same time, Sophia heard a click.

The door sprang open. A cry from within, then tears of delight and relief and gratitude. The old woman's arms around the younger girl, helping her out into the room. Weeping, comforting, reassuring Perdita that no one was hurt, no one had been killed. The old nurse explaining that her husband had gone with the soldiers in exchange for his household being spared.

For the past hour, the servants had been searching the house and grounds. No one knew if she might also have been taken by the soldiers, or that she might have fled and fallen into the river in the dark, slipping through the ice. Then older servants remembered rumours of a hidden room within the house, known only to Lord Lovell.

Perdita inclined her head. Her husband had told her of the room, fearing the anger of the king, and sent her there. Had wanted to keep his new bride safe.

Sophia saw a shadow cross Perdita's face and knew she was thinking of her husband, sacrificing himself to save his family. To save her. As she watched the old woman and her charge, their heads bent low, she realised their voices were becoming more faint. Little by little, their features were fading, their outlines almost transparent now.

She knew her time was done. The story had been rewritten and she had no further part to play. Sophia felt something shift inside her, a sense of the past drifting out of reach and her own time calling her back.

Then, at the very last moment before the connection was broken, Perdita lifted her head and looked straight to where Sophia was standing. And she smiled.

*

Sophia looked down at the yellow scarf in her hand, then slowly walked back down the stairs of the tower and out into the gardens that lay stretched out once more beneath the blue October sky. Minster Lovell Hall was in its ruined state again, no walls or doors or windows to be seen. The trees along the banks of the River Windrush were touched by the copper and burgundy hues of autumn. Soon, though not quite yet, they would start to lose their leaves.

Sophia heard the chimes of the church bell striking midday. On the cobbled path ahead, she saw her companions walking back up towards the coach. She waved and called out that she'd join them in a couple of minutes. Not to go without her.

There was one task remaining.

She walked quickly back along the avenue of trees to the chapel and went inside. It felt different this time, as if she belonged there. She walked up the nave to the altar and looked at the face of the girl – her ancestor – carved in bas-relief. Was she imagining it, but was her expression different now? Sophia lingered there for a few moments more, then turned. Her guidebook was still lying on the pew at the back of the chapel where she had left it earlier.

Sophia opened the book and saw there was more about the Lovell family than she had realised.

Lady Perdita Lovell had been married at Minster Lovell Hall on Christmas Eve 1485. Her husband's life spared by Henry VII, though his lands were forfeit, they had a long and happy marriage and been blessed with many children and grandchildren. Descendants of the Lovell family were still to be found in Oxfordshire, Suffolk and Sussex today.

Sophia closed the book.

As she left the chapel for the last time, she looked up. Now beneath the inscription were the names of Lovell and his bride and their dates. Both had lived long into old age. The scratched letters – LOST BUT NOT FORGOTTEN – were no longer there.

Sophia smiled. Then, tying her yellow scarf around her neck, she stepped out into the autumn sunshine.

Author's Note

This is the second story inspired by the folktale. Following in the footsteps of Samuel Rogers, other authors took up the challenge of writing versions of 'The Mistletoe Bride'. Charles Somerset produced a play of the same name in 1835, Henry James wrote 'The Romance of Certain Old Clothes' in 1868, transposed to eighteenth-century Massachusetts but clearly inspired by the story, and Susan E. Wallace published a short story – 'Ginevra or The Old Oak Chest: A Christmas Story' – in 1887. The tragic tale, a favourite of the protagonist, Brandon Shaw, is recounted in Hitchcock's 1948 film, *Rope*. Jeanette Winterson wrote a haunting Christmas version of the story in 2002.

The song, too, has become part of our literary heritage, appearing, amongst other places, in Thomas Hardy's 1881 novel, *A Laodicean*. In 1859, it was described as 'a national occurrence at Christmas' and, a few years later in 1862, hailed as 'one of the most popular ... ever written.' In the 1970s, I had a copy in an old music hall songbook. With its tripping six-eight beat in A major, and its simple and rousing refrain, it was easy to learn and easy to play. Only now can I see how hopelessly at odds were its catchy lyrics and rhythm and its tragic subject.

There is now an excellent guidebook to Minster Lovell Hall published by English Heritage, but this version was inspired by the moment in the 1970s when I first came upon the legend. Those who've visited the real Minster Lovell Hall will know there was a private family chapel within the north building not in the park. I have made several other changes to the topography for the sake of the story.

SYRINX

A southern market town in Hampshire
The Present Day

Author's Note

Syrinx was commissioned by Sandi Toksvig as part of a series to show theatre – live – on television. It was an ambitious and ground-breaking project, enthusiastically embraced by Sky Arts – two production crews, one theatre team and one television team – with a very specific brief: the plays could have no more than four characters, they had to be set in the present day and had to last twenty-seven minutes!

I had not written a play before, though had long wanted to, and I loved the process of rehearsals, watching the actors inhabit their characters and bring them to life, then going home every night to do rewrites. I was lucky to have a generous and supportive cast and the expert support of both Sandi herself and the director, Patrick Sandford. Robin Don's beautiful design – a ring of school chairs suspended from the rig and a brilliant way of having water on stage – brought the rather drab setting of a headteacher's office in a school to life.

Watching the first performance was both one of the most exhilarating experiences of my professional life and the most terrifying. When the music started – a fragment from Debussy's haunting piece of flute music, 'Syrinx', from which the piece gets its title – my legs started to shake and carried on shaking for the entire twenty-seven minutes. As a novelist, although you see people reading your book – on a train, on a plane, in a café – you can't really tell what they are thinking. Their emotions, reactions, are hidden from you and, besides, it's often a long time after you finished writing, so you're no longer quite so raw. With a play, especially at its first performance, the writer is aware of everyone in the audience and how they are reacting, for good or bad. Since its premiere, the play has had many amateur performances, the first being from the Lapworth Players in May 2011.

*

The first performance was given on 15th July 2009 as part of Sky Arts Theatre Live! at the Sky Television Studios, London.

Marion . . . . Penelope Beaumont
Susan . . . . Sian Thomas
Sarah. . . . . Eleanor Tomlinson
Julie. Gabrielle Lloyd
Director . . . . Patrick Sandford
Creative Producer . . . . Sandi Toksvig
Designer . . . . Robin Don
Production . . . . The Company Presents

Syrinx

27-minute one-act play by Kate Mosse
commissioned by Sky Arts

TIME

The present. Summer. Late afternoon/early evening.

LOCATION

The headteacher's office of a large comprehensive school in a
small southern market town. Downstage right is a desk, tidy,
neat piles of paper and a photograph in a frame. On the corner
of the desk, drinks are laid out – two bottles of red wine, four
bottles of white wine, a couple of cartons of value orange juice,
two bottles of own brand water and eight glasses. The 'door'
into the office from the corridor is downstage left.

CAST (in order of appearance)

MARION KNOWLES – Headteacher
Has been Head of the 1500-student mixed comprehensive school
– her old school – for fifteen years. This is her last year in charge,
having opted for early retirement.

SUSAN WINSTON – Counsellor
A contemporary of Marion's – an old schoolfriend – she too returned to her old home town about ten years ago. She now works as a counsellor at the local Citizens Advice Bureau (CAB) office. Divorced, she has two daughters – one (Phoebe) is just going into her final year of university, the other (Emily) has just taken her A levels and is being presented with a prize this evening.

SARAH PETERS – Dead Girl
Sarah Peters died in a road accident at the age of 18, in the autumn term of her upper sixth year at school. She cannot be seen or heard by the other characters on stage. She was a promising flautist and had auditioned for the Guildhall School of Music. She was best friend to Susan's eldest daughter, Phoebe.

JULIE PETERS – Parent Governor
Mother of Sarah, also a contemporary and schoolfriend of Marion and Susan. Once Susan's closest friend, Julie works part time and is a regular churchgoer. Julie has two other children, two sons.

SCENE 1

Headteacher's Office 6.30 p.m.

The scene opens with a spotlight on Marion, sitting at her desk with her back to the audience. The rest of the set is dark. She is looking at a photograph on her desk. She puts it down, then turns in her chair to face the audience.

MARION: There are moments – in the middle of a busy day or at the dusty tail-end of an autumn afternoon – when, just for an instant, everything stops. Time loses its step and falters. Then the past rushes in. Just in that moment, you see it all clearly, painted in vivid colours, the angles sharp. *(Pauses)* All the things one meant to do and did not, the decisions taken. *(Pause)* Memory has a trick of flattening the complexities of life into a single story until they make sense. Most of it, one can live with, the good and the bad and the indifferent. The account balances out in the end.

But there's always something. One thing. The one mistake that, however hard we try, we cannot let go. That we brood about in the solitary small hours. 'If only I had done this.' 'If only I had not done that.'

If only . . .

Marion looks around. As she does so, lights come up to reveal the whole office. When she speaks, it's with her official voice. *(Picks up a piece of paper from the desk, the speech she's going to give at tonight's prize-giving)*

Ladies and gentlemen, blah, blah, blah. Welcome to this evening's annual prize-giving. As many of you know, I was appointed Head here – my old school, as it happens – twelve years ago. (*Smiles wryly*) About the same time that a certain Tony Blair and his family were given the keys to their new home. My shortcomings, I think I might say, are rather less significant than his. Ha, ha, ha. (*Resumes in speech voice*) However, I am delighted to say that, since 1997 . . .

(*Returns to reflection*) Whatever else, I can truthfully say I am leaving the school in a better state than I found it. It's all here, of course. (*Taps speech*) Yes, it's all here. The facts and figures proving how everything is better now. When all the parents really want to know is: 'Is my child happy? Is she safe? Is she . . .'

A knock jolts Marion out of her reverie. She puts down the paper, stands up and straightens her skirt, takes a final glance around.

SCENE 2

MARION: Come in.

Susan enters.

SUSAN: Oh God, am I the first?

MARION: (*Warmly*) Susan, hello. Come in.

SUSAN: I'm not too early?

MARION: No, no, not at all. I was just going over my speech.

Marion submits to being air-kissed by Susan.

SUSAN: Making sure you go out on a high?

MARION: Something of the kind. (*She moves to the drinks table*) What can I get you? White wine? Red? Orange juice?

Susan hesitates, then replies with a touch of defiance.

SUSAN: White, please. Just a small one.

Marion pours Susan a glass, and water for herself.

SUSAN: So, what's the timetable for tonight?

MARION: The usual, but with bells and whistles, since it's my last one. We've got a girl, a flautist, going off to the Royal Academy in September who's going to play Debussy's 'Syrinx' (*Looks to Susan for a reaction – there is none*).

SUSAN: It sounds lovely. You're not having one?

MARION: Maybe later. And then the choir has prepared something special.

SUSAN: God, the choir! We were the tallest, so we were always made to stand at the back in concerts. (*Grins*)

MARION: You kept sticking your tongue out at someone in the orchestra.

SUSAN: Just livening things up a bit!

MARION: You were a terror! You could have been a prefect, top of the class, if you'd put your mind to it. If you hadn't been so determined to be different. I was always surprised you and Julie were such good friends. *(Susan's face clouds over. Marion ploughs on).* You couldn't have been less like each other. She was always so anxious and polite, always in the library working hard, church on Sundays.

SUSAN: Maybe it was because we were so different that we got on so well. There was no pressure, if you know what I mean, no competition between us.

MARION: *(Quietly)* I'm not sure that's how Julie felt.

SUSAN: Well, it's all in the past now.

MARION: And so she married Paul, s*tayed* married.

SUSAN: Whereas I . . .

MARION: *(Finishing the thought)* . . . vanished to Morocco with a gorgeous but rather unreliable artist. We were all so jealous! What was he called?

SUSAN: Konrad. Tall blond German junkie! *(Laughs)* My God, if either of my girls tried to pull a stunt like that.

MARION: Emily and Phoebe are both too level-headed for that!

SUSAN: Unlike their mother, you mean. It's odd, you know, but I feel quite at home here.

MARION: Well you did spend rather a lot of time in this office!

SUSAN: *(Laughs)* When I left, I vowed never to set foot inside this establishment ever again. I hated it! Now look at me. Both the girls have gone through the school – and loved it – and here we are, after all these years, to give you a great send-off.

You think you're going to miss it? Any regrets?

MARION: Of course I'll miss it. Some of it. But, off the record, on balance I'll be glad to go. I've done my time. We don't teach properly any more, it's all tests and more tests. We don't equip them to think for themselves. *(Pauses)* And the parents. God, the parents! Half of them couldn't give a damn, the other half living their children's lives for them.

Marion pulls herself up short, realising she's going on.

SUSAN: But you've made such a success of it, Marion. I'm so proud of you.

MARION: *(Marion goes to desk to pick up photo. Tone lightens)* I found it when I was clearing things out.

SUSAN: My God, we look so young. I remember that day. The three of us setting out on a 'proper' walk, as you put it.

MARION: You, me and Julie.

SUSAN: Yes. You, of course, had organised the whole
           thing like a military operation. Made us trudge
           up Bury Hill, lugging a whole load of picnic stuff
           with us.

MARION: You complained most of the time. *(Puts on a
           child's voice)* 'My rucksack's too heavy'. Julie ended
           up carrying most of your things as well as her
           own. I never did understand why she put up with
           you!

SUSAN: *(Quietly)* No.

SCENE 3

Each of Sarah's soliloquies is delivered with her visible on stage.
Unless specified, other characters do not react to her presence
and remain motionless on stage.

SARAH: She knew, Miss Knowles. She knew and she did
           nothing. She saw us, you see, walking by the river.
           October. Not holding hands, or anything. Just
           talking, but she called me in to her office the next
           day. Came straight out with it. That Matt – Mr
           Grahame, she called him – was a teacher and I was
           a pupil and that was that. The fact that Matt was
           only a student teacher and wasn't even working at
           my school any more . . . He was a musician really.
           A pianist. Really good.

           Anyway, she told me to think about the damage
           it might do to his reputation. And what my mum
           would say – Miss Knowles and my mum and

Phoebe's mum, Susan – they all went to school together a million years ago. She said Mum didn't believe in that kind of thing. *(Blushes)* As if I didn't know!

Then she said she knew what it was like to be young. Yeah, right! She would turn a blind eye, she said, provided she had my word that the *affair* stopped – that's the word she used, affair.

But I couldn't give her my word because Matt was amazing. So totally amazing. *(Smiles)* He called me his syrinx, because that was the piece I was playing when he first noticed me. *(Giggles)* After he said it, I went straight online and looked it up. Gods v mortals, all very Greek. It turned out syrinx was some kind of water nymph. Pan fancied her, but she wasn't interested. Vanished into the river and hid among the reeds to get out of it. *(Pauses)* I'd been practising the piece for ages, but for the first time I wanted to know what it meant.

So, you see, I couldn't promise I wouldn't see him again, because well, without Matt, there wouldn't be any point. I was happy. Really happy. And, it was weird, but Miss Knowles never mentioned it again, well not until the funeral. But by then it was too late. *(Pauses)* She was all right. *(Pauses)* It wasn't her fault.

SCENE 4

Action resumes as if there had been no interruption. Susan is still holding photograph.

SUSAN: Wasn't this the day you announced your aim was to write a guidebook to the walks of Sussex? The only problem, you had to do them all first!

MARION: And I still haven't done even half of them. Life got in the way. Hence getting out of here while I still have it in me.

SUSAN: Before your knees give out.

MARION: As you say, before my knees give out.

          Susan, how are things?

SUSAN: Things have been very busy at work.

MARION: *(Quietly)* I didn't mean work.

SUSAN: I know you didn't.

MARION: So?

SUSAN: Not now. This is your night.

MARION: But I'd rather—

SUSAN: Really, Marion. I don't want to talk about it.

MARION: So how is the world of counselling?

SUSAN: Fabulous! Mostly debt and bankruptcy counselling, these days. Very depressing. *(Seeing*

Marion's expression) Don't worry, I'm sticking with
it. I'm just a bit done in at the moment.

MARION: And that's why I wanted to talk to you—

SUSAN: *(Continuing her train of thought)* On the upside, the
girls are both great. Emily's getting a prize, and
Phoebe's loving Manchester.

MARION: *(Accepting she's again missed her moment)* And after
she's finished?

SUSAN: Who knows? Trying to get a job in this climate,
not easy.

MARION: I'm sure she'll be fine.

SUSAN: Phoebe's more fragile than she looks. She's been
fine at uni – well, once she found her feet – but I
worry she'll run into difficulties again. Not cope.

MARION: It was a long time ago, Susan.

SUSAN: Three years. Hardly any time.

MARION: Long time for a teenage girl. *(Susan doesn't answer)*
You've got to stop feeling guilty. Put it behind you
and move on, isn't that what you'd be telling your
clients to do? Letting go, not getting stuck.

Susan doesn't respond.

MARION: It's not about Phoebe really, is it? It's about you.
You've got to forgive yourself, Susan. You've—

SUSAN: *(Snapping)* No, Marion. Not now. Really. I don't
want to talk about it. It's hard enough being here

as it is. If it wasn't for the fact Emily's getting a prize – and that it's your last one, of course – I wouldn't have come.

The two women stare at one another. Action freezes.

SCENE 5

SARAH: I told Phoebe. I had to tell someone.

The funny thing was, Phoebe wasn't surprised. She told me she'd seen him outside the music room one day. I didn't know he was there, listening. Phoebe said when I finished, Matt closed his eyes. Like it was too much to bear. She thought it was sweet. Romantic.

So, Phoebe knew. She knew before I knew. Phoebe's brilliant! We met at her house, sometimes, when her mum was out. *(Thinking aloud – a diversion)* They're so like each other, Susan and Phoebe. Susan's awesome. She's totally mad, but she's a good laugh. But she's my mum's best mate and Mum had found out and was freaking out as it was.

We were doing OK, Matt and I, until that night. November. I'd arranged to go round to Phoebe's. Matt was doing a gig and it was over-21s so I couldn't go, and Susan was at a party. Me and Phoebe hadn't had a girls' night in for ages and there was stuff *(looks embarrassed)* I needed to talk to her about.

Well, it's over now. And Phoebe still hasn't told. It wasn't her fault. Wasn't Susan's fault.

SCENE 6

There's another knock at the door.

JULIE: Sorry, am I interrupting?

A thin, anxious-looking woman walks on stage.

MARION: Julie, come in, come in. It's lovely you could make it.

The woman walks towards Marion, then stops when she sees Susan. Julie and Susan stare at each other, neither able to believe the other is there. For a moment, it looks as if Julie will make a bolt for the door. But Marion puts an arm around her and steers her to the centre of the room.

SUSAN: Julie, I had no idea you'd be here. I—

MARION: *(Still with her arm around Julie's waist)* Can I get you something to drink, Julie? A glass of wine.

JULIE: *(Her voice is brittle)* Nothing, thank you.

MARION: We have orange juice, if you'd prefer a soft drink. Fizzy water?

JULIE: *(Looking towards the door)* I'm fine. Thank you.

The intercom goes. Marion answers.

MARION: Sorry? Okay, I'm coming.

          I'm sorry, it seems I'm indispensable. I won't be more than a couple of minutes.

JULIE: I don't want—

MARION: *(Interrupting)* Julie, I need a governor's signature
         on a couple of things. If you could just hang on
         here a moment. I'll be as quick as I can.

SUSAN: Marion, I don't think it's—

But Marion has gone. The sound of a flautist warming up –
playing scales – slips through the door, then the door shuts.

SCENE 7

There is a long, hard silence. Julie stands with her hand
clutching the strap of her shoulder bag. Susan, caught halfway between the door and the table, doesn't know what to do.
She's pleased to see Julie and obviously very nervous. A minute
passes, neither woman speaking or catching each other's eye.
Julie pointedly looks at the glass, but says nothing. Susan puts
her glass down on the desk.

SUSAN: It's good to see you. *(Pause)* You look well.

JULIE: *(Polite)* So do you.

SUSAN: And the family? Paul and the boys? They're well?

JULIE: They are all fine.

SUSAN: Mark's working full-time at the marina, I think
         someone told me?

JULIE: Yes.

SUSAN: Hard to get a permanent job there, I'd have
         thought. You must be very proud of him.

JULIE: I am.

SUSAN: And Stephen?

JULIE: He's getting a prize this evening. *(Her tone changes from polite to aggressive)* It was inevitable I'd be here, wasn't it?

SUSAN: *(Confused by the non sequitur)* I'm sorry?

JULIE: *(Accusingly)* You said you'd no idea I'd be here. But I am a governor. Obviously I'd be here. Or maybe you don't bother to read the newsletter. You probably don't know who any of the governors are. *(Looks at Susan)*.

SUSAN: *(Flustered)* No, I did. Do know, that is.

JULIE: If you had known I'd be here, would you have stayed away?

SUSAN: No. I mean, yes. That is, I meant Marion hadn't told me you'd be coming. Here, first, I mean.

JULIE: So you're saying you wouldn't have come?

SUSAN: I, I don't know. That is, Emily's up for a prize too. It's great about Stephen, although I'm not surprised. He's an outstanding sportsman by all accounts.

JULIE: It's for music.

SUSAN: *(Even more bothered)* Oh. Right. I didn't realise he – as well as . . .

JULIE: As well as Sarah, were you going to say?

SUSAN: Yes, Emily says Stephen's in every team going. But, music. That's great. Well done him.

She grinds to a halt, realising she's making things worse.

JULIE: How's Phoebe?

SUSAN: *(Giving up the pretence of polite conversation)* Please. Don't do this.

JULIE: Do what? You ask after my family. I ask after yours. That's what we do in awkward social situations, isn't it, make small talk? *(Gives a tight smile)* Is she enjoying university?

SUSAN: *(Seeing no way out)* She is. She's fine.

JULIE: And she's recovered? No more problems.

Susan glances at the door, then at Julie. She is clearly trying to come to a decision of some kind. Susan decides she's got nothing to lose.

SUSAN: Julie, look. *(Julie turns away. Susan carries on anyway)* Look. I – I know there's nothing I can say, nothing I can do to make up for what happened. Believe me, I think about it every day.

Susan reaches out for Julie's arm. Julie shrugs her off.

SUSAN: But can't we at least talk? Can't we see if . . .

JULIE: *(Spins round to face her)* See if what, Susan? If—

SCENE 8

The door opens and Marion reappears. Feeling the tension between them, she hesitates a moment, worried her plan to at least get the two old friends together in the same room was a mistake.

MARION: They're ready for us. Shall we?

Both women glare at her. Caught by the need to put a brave face on it for their children's sakes, at first neither woman moves. Then Julie walks briskly past Susan, and exits.

SUSAN: Why didn't you tell me you'd invited Julie too? Here. Beforehand.

MARION: I tried to, but—

SUSAN: It's just making everything worse.

Susan exits. Marion hesitates, a worried look on her face, then goes to the desk, picks up her speech. She puts on her official face and follows them out. Offstage, the sound of chairs scraping back. The orchestra strikes up and the choir begins to sing.

SCENE 9

SARAH: They all feel guilty, responsible. But for stuff they didn't do.

If only. Such pointless words.

Me and Mum argued that night. Again. It wasn't like her to lose it, not really. I guess I just flipped out too. Why couldn't she see I was happy? Why couldn't she be happy for me? She started up about homework and college and church! She didn't understand I wasn't a kid any more.

We never got the chance to make up. We never got the chance to say sorry for all the stuff we said that night. And, *(looks at Julie)* look, she can't forgive herself for that. I saw it on her face at the funeral. At the inquest. In church. Standing outside my empty room at the top of the stairs. My brothers tiptoeing around her. For once, thinking about someone else's feelings. Amazing!

But it was an accident. It had started to rain, so I rang Matt and he left the gig and came and got me. But it wasn't your fault.

Offstage, we hear the announcement of the next item, a round of applause, then the sound of a single flautist playing the beginning of Debussy's 'Syrinx'. As the sound of the flute filters into the office. Sarah smiles, as Julie comes back onto stage, looking anguished.

SCENE 10

The same location. Later the same evening.

Julie is sitting alone in the dark. Marion comes in, leaving the door ajar. She turns on the light on the desk and doesn't notice Julie is there.

JULIE: No. Please leave it.

MARION: Julie. You gave me a shock.

She dims the light.

MARION: I saw you go out. *(Pause)* I thought you'd gone home.

JULIE: I intended to, but then. *(Pause)* It's quiet here.

MARION: I can go if you'd rather be alone?

JULIE: No. No, it's all right. Stay. *(Long pause)* It was that piece – 'Syrinx' – Sarah's piece – I couldn't bear to hear it. Played here. By someone else. *(Pulls herself together)* Did the rest of it go off all right?

MARION: Yes.

JULIE: Where are the others?

MARION: There are drinks in the hall.

JULIE: *(Interrupting)* Susan too?

MARION: I think so, with Emily.

Marion puts her speech back down on her desk.

JULIE: *(In a low voice)* We argued that night, Sarah and I. Not for the first time. Always the same subject. *(Looks at Marion)* I knew they met here first, you know.

MARION: I give you my word that nothing—

JULIE: *(Waves her hand)* I know it didn't start here. Sarah told me. But he was too old for her. She stopped coming to church, you know. Paul said if we put up opposition it would make Sarah more determined. He thought we should let it run its course. *(Shakes her head)* I didn't listen.

MARION: You can't blame yourself. She was eighteen. Not a child. She was happy.

JULIE: *(Gives a bitter laugh)* Happy!

MARION: You could see it. Everything about Sarah changed. She was doing so well, in her music, her lessons, everything. She had a kind of lightness to her that transformed the world around her. *(Quietly)* I know her choice might not have been your choice, Julie, but she was happy.

JULIE: Happy! And what good did it do her?

SCENE 11

Susan's voice is heard in the corridor outside.

SUSAN: *(Offstage)* I'll just say goodbye, Emily. Wait for me in the hall.

Susan comes smiling into the room, then stops dead when she sees Marion and Julie.

SUSAN: I'm sorry. I didn't mean to barge in. I just wanted to . . .

Marion beckons her in. Julie gets up. She doesn't want Susan to see her upset.

JULIE: I'm just leaving.

SUSAN: No. Don't go on my account.

MARION: I don't think either of you should go. *(There's something in her voice that cuts through both Susan and Julie's awkwardness.)* It just seems such a waste. You two. All those years of friendship. The three of us.

Suddenly, both realise Marion has engineered the whole evening. They turn on her.

JULIE: *(Accusingly)* You chose that piece of music deliberately, didn't you?

SUSAN: I can't believe you thought this would be a good idea. What did you think, Marion, that we could just forget the last three years? For old time's sake?

MARION: *(Steadfast)* It's gone on too long. You two should talk. Start talking, at least. Before it's too late. See if—

JULIE: See if what? What, Marion? If you can bring Sarah back? See if we can gloss over the fact that she *(she points at Susan)* killed my daughter?

SUSAN: *(At breaking point)* But that's not how it was. You know that's not how it was. The coroner, everyone, said it wasn't my fault. He – Matt – lost control of the car in the rain. The river had come up over the road. I swerved to avoid them, he skidded and hit the wall and . . . well. There was nothing I could do. Julie, believe me—

JULIE: *(Interrupting)* You walked away without a scratch.

SUSAN: That's not true. I was in hospital for—

JULIE: *(Not listening)* You'd been drinking.

SUSAN: One glass. I wasn't over the limit.

JULIE: *(Twisting the crucifix at her neck between her fingers.)* Don't you dare tell me it was only one glass! Don't you dare! Have you forgotten I was the one who sat with you night after night after Pete had left you? It was me that stopped the girls seeing you drunk, clearing away the bottles. So don't you dare tell me it was just one glass!

SUSAN: That was then. A few months, that's all. Never again. Never since then.

MARION: Julie ...

JULIE: *(Ignoring Marion)* But what if that one glass of wine dulled your reactions? What if, because of that one glass of wine, you weren't quick enough, sharp enough? It might have made the difference.

MARION: You know it wouldn't. The coroner was quite clear that there was nothing Susan could have done. You heard him say it.

SUSAN: *(Wearily)* It doesn't matter. I don't want to argue.

MARION: Look. In one way or another, we all feel responsible. *(They both look at her)* Yes, all of us. It's hard, I know it's hard. Phoebe lost her best friend. Do you two have to lose each other as well? Susan is wracked by guilt, I—

JULIE: *(Interrupting)* Poor Susan, poor Phoebe, poor
            Marion. But what about Sarah? What about me?

MARION: Matt swerved and lost control and he died. Like
            Sarah, he died and left you with no one to blame.
            Julie, I'm only saying that if you could accept it
            was an accident, that it wasn't Susan's fault, then
            perhaps *you*—

JULIE: *(Turning on her)* Whose fault is it then? Mine?
            Is that what you're saying?

SUSAN: *(Simultaneously)* No one thinks that.

MARION: *(Simultaneously)* Of course not.

JULIE: *(Turning on Marion)* What about you? You knew
            about it, didn't you? You had a duty of care. She
            was a pupil. He was a teacher. A member of your
            staff. You should have done something.

MARION: He wasn't. Not by then. *(Pauses)* I did my best.
            You know I did. I talked to her. There wasn't
            anything else I could do.

JULIE: There was plenty you could have done. There
            are rules about that sort of thing, a relationship
            between a pupil and a teacher. Aren't there?
            (Marion doesn't answer) Well, aren't there?

MARION: *(Deliberately)* He had left the school. He wasn't her
            teacher. I didn't think I had the right to interfere.

JULIE: No. You chose not to. For reasons of your own, you
            chose to do nothing. And because of you – and

you *(to Susan)* – my child is dead. My daughter is dead. So when you tell me, Marion, we should talk, I say to you, what is there to talk about? What is there to talk about, tell me that?

Marion tries to put her hand on Julie's arm.

JULIE: Don't.

SCENE 12

SARAH: I really loved him, Mum. He was amazing. We'd got it all worked out. I'd get my A levels out the way, then go to college – Guildhall, fingers crossed – and he'd get a job in London. It'd be perfect.

        But, I loved you too, Mum. I never meant for this to happen. Love you.

SCENE 13

Action resumes. Julie looks at the space where Sarah was standing, as if she heard her.

JULIE: Sarah said she'd done her homework, and was going over to Phoebe's. *(Julie turns to Susan)* She said you knew. Were expecting her. *(Susan nods)* I didn't believe her. Accused her of being deceitful, of lying so she could sneak out to see him. Said awful things.

        I waited for her to come back. Angry – and then worried. Oh, not really. Just like you do. It started to rain really hard and I – I didn't know where she was, I didn't know. *(Pauses)* She called him. Called him. Called him to come and get her. Him, not me.

It was easier to hate you than to hate myself. To make it your fault. Somebody else's fault. There was a part of me that was actually pleased when Phoebe became ill – depressed – because it seemed only fair. Such evil thoughts. And this did – does – nothing. God doesn't help. All those prayers I say don't help me to make sense of things. Just words. They don't help me to accept or forgive. *(Looks at Susan)* And you? The one person who in other circumstances I would turn to? The one person I couldn't bear to be near.

Susan leans over and touches Julie's arm. This time, she does not shrug her off. Susan holds the position a moment, then withdraws her hand.

SUSAN: I relive that night over and over in my mind. If only I hadn't gone to that party. If only I'd stayed here with Phoebe. If only it hadn't been me behind the wheel. If only.

MARION: *(An echo of her earlier speech)* If only I had put a stop to it. I suppose, there was part of me that rejoiced to see her so confident, suddenly, so sure of herself. She was a different girl – young woman. When I looked at her and saw her so radiant, I couldn't bring myself to spoil it.

JULIE: *(Weary)* It wasn't your decision to make.

MARION: *(Quietly)* But was it yours?

All three fall silent for a moment. Sarah looks at each of them in turn.

SUSAN: *(To Julie)* I miss you.

JULIE: *(Catches her breath)* I miss you. I do miss you, but it's too hard. When I look at you, I see only what I've lost.

SUSAN: I understand.

JULIE: It wasn't your fault. I do know that. *(Looks to Marion)* Or yours.

SUSAN: Can you forgive me? That it was me?

JULIE: I don't know. I don't know. *(Her hand goes to the crucifix at her neck)*.

Slowly, the light fades, leaving only a spotlight on the photograph on the desk for a few seconds. For a moment, Sarah's face is visible backstage centre, as if watching over the older women. She is smiling. Then, fade to black.

Acknowledgements

I'd like to thank everyone at LAW, ILA and Inkwell Management who give such expert advice and care – in particular Alice Saunders, Nicki Kennedy, Sam Edenborough and Mark Lucas, for his endless time, good company . . . and *those* electronic notes!

At Orion, there's a wonderful team of hard working, enthusiastic, energetic people – too many to name everyone – but special mention must go to Jon Wood, Genevieve Pegg, Eleanor Dryden, Laura Gerrard, Anthony Keates, Gaby Young, copy editor Liz Hatherell, the fantastic sales forces (both in-house and on the road), the art department and Rohan Eason for his beautiful and atmospheric illustrations. Last, but by no means least, the force of nature that is Susan Lamb!

I'm also very appreciative of the support of my publishers all over the world – especially Isabelle Laffont at Lattès, Annette Weber at Droemer-Knaur, Cathrine Bakke Bolin at Gyldendal, Rachel Kahan at Morrow (for Governors Island and much else), Frederika van Traa at Unieboek – and everyone at Hachette Australia, Hachette New Zealand, Hachette Canada and Jonathan Ball in South Africa.

I'd like to thank the following publishers for their permission to use the following quotations: W.W.Norton for lines from 'Dispossessions' by Jane Cooper, Yale University Press for lines from 'A Bride's Hours' by Jean Valentine and Faber and Faber for lines from 'Church Going' by Philip Larkin and 'The Dry Salvages' by T.S. Eliot.

Finally, as always, my love and gratitude to my family and friends who are patient and always proud, despite the number of hours I spend hidden away and avoiding the washing up! My mother Barbara and my mother-in-law Rosie, but most of all Greg, Martha and Felix. I couldn't do it – any of it – without you.